TRUSTING
JAKE

Elite Security Mystery, Book 1

BARBARA MCMAHON

One

He'd found her. The quiet satisfaction went deep. He'd been looking for her for more than eighteen months. A couple of times he'd wondered if she were dead, but each time he'd picked up a new lead that led to another. And convinced him she was alive.

Now she sat right in front of him, four tables over, sharing lunch with three friends. He could scarcely believe the end was in sight. He dropped his gaze to his menu, knowing he was out of her line of sight, but wanting nothing to spook her. People could tell when someone was watching them.

Casually he glanced her way again. She'd have to pass by his table to leave. There was no other way out of the cafe. For the moment, he could relax. He'd have to turn his head when she was ready to leave, but he doubted she'd even glance his way.

She'd changed since the last time he'd seen her. She was laughing at something one of the other women was saying and the sparkling lights in her blue eyes brought forth an old memory--of the morning he'd located her in Baltimore a dozen years ago.

She looked as happy today as she had then. The

years had changed her obviously. She'd put on some weight and cut her silky blonde hair. The jeans and flannel shirt were a marked dissimilarity from the designer gowns she'd worn years ago. Somehow the casual outfit suited her. Maybe it was because of the surroundings, the similar attire of the other people in the café. Last time he'd seen her she'd been enveloped by diamonds and satin.

If anyone had asked before today, he'd have thought she'd stick out like a sore thumb in this small Colorado mountain community. Seeing her with her friends, she fit in as if she'd lived here forever.

Jake sighed softly. He'd found her again--she wasn't going to like it–again. More than eighteen months of investigation and now only twelve feet separated them-- that and the diner's customers.

Jake shifted his chair so he could watch her from the corner of his eye. He counted on her being so involved with the others at her table that she wouldn't think to look around. He didn't know if she'd recognize him if she spotted him, it had been eight years since she'd last seen him.

Eight years! Where did the time go? The older he got, the faster it went. He'd kept tabs on her during the first years after Baltimore. Idly he wondered if her grandfather knew that? Mentally he shrugged. It didn't matter. It didn't hurt for a mouse to look at a queen.

And the treatment they'd found for her must have worked. She looked healthy and normal from where he sat.

Wryly he almost smiled. Despite her fervent

teenaged beliefs, no one had killed her twelve years ago. Or any time since.

"What'll you have?" A young waitress slapped down a napkin and silverware. She pulled an order pad from her apron pocket and stood waiting, slowly chewing gum. Her fresh face a reminder of the first time he'd gone after Kassie. She'd been about this girl's age back then.

"Apple pie and coffee." He didn't know how long Kassie *Montgomery* would take to finish lunch but he didn't plan to leave a full meal behind to cause comment if she left soon.

For a minute Jake considered confronting her here in the restaurant. But he'd been patient all these months, he could wait until she was alone. It would be better to confront her at home, away from her friends. Away from any entanglements or interference. She wasn't going to be happy to see him and he didn't have the law on his side this time to enforce her return.

He was just going to take her back.

Waiting for the pie, he glanced out the window at the softly falling snow. It had begun as he reached the outskirts of town an hour ago. If he didn't make his move soon, they might not make Denver before dark. If the prediction for the storm held, they'd be stuck in this hole-in-the-wall town for the night, if not longer. He frowned. Maybe he should approach her now, get this show on the road.

The waitress smiled when she returned with his slice of pie, turning the plate to make sure the tip pointed directly at his chest. She set down the coffee and a small pitcher of cream. "That it?" she asked.

"Looks fine," he said. So much for apprehending Kassie Montgomery immediately. He'd eat the pie first, keep an eye on her. She wasn't going far. He knew where she lived, where she worked, what name she was using. He'd catch her at home. Then after a few hours flying time he'd deliver her to her grandfather once again. Was it starting to become a habit?

Kassie Montgomery laughed at the punch line. Philip always came up with the most outrageous blond jokes to share, and teasingly held her eye every time. The two other women at their table, Mary and Eileen, also laughed. Philip's jokes were always funny--though she accused him often of scrounging the world for blonde jokes on her account.

Suddenly Kassie's amusement faded. The hair on the back of her neck prickled. She shivered uneasily for the first time in years. It felt as if someone watched her. Slowly she let her gaze drift around the coffee shop. None of the other diners seemed to be paying any attention to the group at her table. She glanced out the window. No one there.

"Oops, look at the snow. I've got to be going," she said, fully aware of the storm for the first time. The weatherman had been predicting a blizzard for two days. "You know they don't plow my road until last. If I don't want to spend the entire holidays camped out with one of you, I'd better get home."

"So you can be snowed in for Christmas?" Mary

asked, pulling up her purse and rummaging in it for her wallet.

"Depending on how bad the storm is and if and when they clear the roads." Kassie shrugged as she, too, found a handful of bills. "I could be. But I have plenty of supplies. And no family to visit. I'll be fine. Besides— two weeks of freedom from the little monsters, be still my beating heart!"

"Thought you were going to come to our place for Christmas Day," Eileen said, looking up when Kassie spoke.

"If I can make it, I'll drop by in the afternoon. But if not, I'll take a rain check. Maybe we'll do the New Year in together. Either way, I'll give you a call. Mostly I want to celebrate two weeks of freedom."

Philip laughed. "You love them as much as we do, Kassie, don't try to con us."

Her expression stilled for a split second, caught at his term. She recovered swiftly, nodded and smiled. These were her friends--fellow teachers at Winter Creek High School. Philip meant nothing with his comment-- he had no idea her whole life was a con. And she'd make damn sure none of them ever found out.

"True. Merry Christmas to each of you." Rising, she hugged each friend as they prepared to depart. With another quick glance around the café, Kassie drew on her down jacket and walked with her friends to the door.

In only moments she turned her four-wheel drive SUV toward home, the heat blasting to keep the keening cold of the icy Colorado winds at bay. The snow fall increased as she drove slower and slower. Dense white flakes swirled and danced in the wind, piling up quickly on the windshield. She put the car in four-wheel drive, not that she needed it yet, but she had no desire to skid off the road into a snow bank at the beginning of Christmas vacation.

It was still early afternoon, but already growing dark with the storm. She flicked on her lights. School had let out at noon for the two-week vacation and she'd gone to a celebratory lunch with her closest friends. She'd be glad to get home, though.

Thunder would be glad to see her, too. The big German Shepherd was lonely while she was away all day. But she never considered changing that. She needed a dog, that dog, to feel safe. Not every teacher had a trained guard dog for a roommate. Not every teacher needed one.

Most of the time, she forgot his training. He was a much loved companion. And how he loved snow. Maybe they could play out in it for a while before dinner. She'd throw snowballs and laugh at his antics trying to find them in the drifts.

Kassie carefully turned off the highway onto the lane that led to her place. Few houses lined the narrow country road. Her house was the farthest from the highway. Two of the houses she passed were closed for winter. The Maguires, in the third house, the one closest to hers, had already left for the Christmas holidays with their daughter in Phoenix.

But the isolation and solitude suited her perfectly. She didn't want to live surrounded by people, hemmed in at every direction--she'd had a surfeit of that under her grandfather's rule. When deciding on a home, she'd chosen her house primarily because of its isolation. The cheap rent hadn't hurt, either. She made ends meet on her salary, even had a little saved up. But no permanent ties for her. Life was too uncertain.

And the strongest selling point of her place had been its escape path.

Her lips tightened momentarily as her thoughts skidded to the old man. It had been months since he'd popped into mind. The dark memories swirled. He'd kept her virtually a prisoner for the last five years she'd lived under his thumb. The sorry bastard. And her dear aunt Beatrice had been just as bad.

Samuel Toggins, her grandfather's secretary, had been the only sympathetic person in the crowd at the house--but had remained loyal to her grandfather in the end. Only Jason had been on her side.

Sometimes she wished she felt safe enough to contact him, to see what he was doing. To let him know she was okay.

But she dare not. She was on her own, living her life exactly as she wished. Grateful she'd never see the old man again, she banished him from her thoughts. She'd done her best to insure he'd never find her. And if by some fluke they did cross paths again, she had her escape planned.

Reaching home, she pulled under the car shed and killed the engine. The hush fell around her as the snow swirled lazily in fat, fluffy flakes, sheltered from the wind in this pocket beneath the tall evergreens.

She shivered a little when she stepped out. The icy

air penetrated her jeans, danced around her neck with its cold fingers. Hurrying to the front door, she was thankful she'd stocked up on food and supplies last week. She'd planned at the time to avoid driving into town during her vacation. Now she didn't need to worry about the weather, or road conditions, she had enough food to last the two weeks. School would resume long before she ran short on anything.

And there was plenty of wood, she thought with a smile as she took an armful of logs from her stash on the sheltered porch. The rest lay beneath tarps in the back, but she kept a huge stack replenished by the door, beneath the porch roof, to keep it dry and handy.

A deep bark greeted her as she fumbled with the key. Throwing open the door, she knew to stand to one side as the sleek black and tan shepherd streaked through and out onto the snow, pausing as his paws sank in the white power, a comical expression of surprise on his face.

"Hello, Thunder." She grinned at him and watched as he scampered around the yard, barking and chasing snowflakes. He was only three, not much more than a pup--with the energy to prove it. But he was full grown, weighing in at 110 pounds, a big German Shepard. And the love of her life.

She closed the door and dumped the wood in the stack next to the stove, then started a fire. The main part of the small log house was heated primarily by the wood burning stove. Electric heaters stood in each of the bedrooms, but she didn't use them unless she had to. Money was scarce, and electrical heating could get costly.

Thunder scratched at the door and she went to let him in, holding him by the door while he shook off the snow, preventing him from dripping on her rugs.

She kept a huge old bath towel near the door for such situations. He was almost dry when she heard the car. Pausing, she tossed the towel down and moved to the window, peering out into the snow storm, trying to see who was approaching. Her friends didn't visit unless they called first. None of them would be coming out on a day like today--the snow fall was predicted in the inches. Was it someone who had lost his way?

Unlikely this far off the main road.

She drew in her breath in startled disbelief as she recognized the driver. Not a face she would ever forget. Jake Lancaster.

Memories crowded as fear rose and threatened to choke her. Then lifesaving anger flared. Instantly every memory of that humiliating day in Baltimore resurfaced. That man was the sole reason she'd been through five years of hell!

She remembered his implacability when she tried to get away, when he'd discovered her after her aborted attempt to escape the domination of the old man. Was he here on his behalf?

She didn't believe in coincidence. Jake Lancaster was nothing but trouble with a capital T.

How had he found her?

Jake climbed out of the car, muttering an expletive as the cold zapped straight through his clothes. Damn, he was hardly dressed for a blizzard. Slowly he walked toward the house, scanning the grounds, listening for any sounds. Her car was beneath a carport. She'd come straight home. Snow crunched beneath his feet. The hush sounded unnatural.

He stopped near the porch, eying the log structure before him. It looked like a dozen other places he'd seen in this part of the country. Rugged, strong, built to last several lifetimes. Plain and functional. A far cry from an antebellum mansion on the Savannah Road outside Atlanta. Too small for servants. How did Sutherland's princess granddaughter manage?

"Not that it matters," he muttered, closing the distance. Time enough to satisfy his curiosity once he got inside. Or she could tell him all about life on the run while they flew back to Atlanta. But first he needed to get out of the blasted cold!

Before he took another step, however, the door opened and she stepped out, a double barrel shotgun leveled at his chest. The pumping action echoed in the muffled snowfall. Jake froze, his gaze locking with hers, recognizing instantly the implacable determination that shone from her blue eyes.

Damn! Little Kassie had grown up.

Seeing him approach her house, Kassie reached for the shotgun. She'd practiced the drill endless times when she'd first arrived. Wanting to be prepared for discovery when it came, as the months passed she'd begun to think she would never be found. Seeing Jake again, however, changed everything. For an instant she let the old anger wash through her, dampening down the fear. How dare he try to invade her life again! Was she never to be left alone?

This time he'd discover she was not a shy teenager unable to resist being led back to virtual prison. This time she was prepared. More prepared than Jake Lancaster expected. And more determined than she'd been at seventeen.

Thunder growled deep in his throat, his hair raised on his back. She opened the door, spoke a word to the dog, and stood in the frame, shotgun pointed directly at Jake Lancaster's chest. Coolly she pumped the action. Used to the weight, she never let the barrel waver.

It had been a dozen years since he'd found her in Baltimore, at least seven or eight since she'd last seen him. He looked the same. Big, powerful, and mean. He wore jeans, flat soled black biker boots and a denim jacket. His dark hair was a little longer, surely no longer regulation for a cop, unless he worked undercover. It was quickly being coated with snow. His eyes met hers, held. Still a dark, smoky blue. Deep and cautious, they gave nothing away.

He wasn't dressed warmly enough for the storm that swirled around him. Let him freeze, she thought with some satisfaction, the gun steady. He stopped in his tracks, raising his hands away from his side. His eyes stared straight into hers.

"Hello Kassie," he said easily, his eyes watchful, alert. He'd not expected the shotgun, that much was evident. Nor the dog growling at her side. A quick glance at the teeth on the animal, then his hard gaze met hers again. He didn't move.

"Get the hell off my property, Lancaster. Or I'll call the cops." Again she remembered Baltimore. The heady taste of freedom had been a rush--one in her innocence she had thought to keep forever. But he'd made sure that hadn't happened. He'd taken the old bastard's money and dragged her back to hell. She would never forget.

But if he was looking for a repeat, he'd be in for a quite a surprise.

"I've come a long way to see you," he said. Snow began to settle on his shoulders, on his head turning his dark hair white. He was still as big as she remembered. His rough-hewn face hadn't aged. Yet he had to be in his middle thirties, maybe older. She knew he was hard, implacable--and capable of selling out to the man with the most money. She dare not underestimate the man.

"I don't want to see you. I sure don't want to talk to you. Did the old man send you?"

"If you mean your grandfather, yes. He wants to see you. He's been worried about you." Plus there were family members pushing to have her declared dead. He'd just proved that impossible.

Jake essayed his chances of getting the gun. How good a shot was she? Not that it mattered. A shotgun had a wide spread. At this distance she couldn't miss. Did she have the nerve to pull the trigger?

It was a moot point. The dog convinced him any chances of rushing her stood between zip and zero.

"Liar," she said, without heat. "He only wants to control me, he could care less beyond that. I'm not seventeen any more Lancaster. And any phony papers saying I'm crazy would be torn up and tossed away. I have too many people who've known me for too long to let that lie get any mileage. Get off my property!"

Jake frowned, glancing at the shotgun. "I've been looking for you for more than eighteen months. Can we at least talk?"

"There's nothing to talk about. Get in your car, turn it around and get. And don't tell him where I am," she said her mind already racing ahead--thoughts tumbling over themselves as she tried to remember all she had to do before leaving.

It was a foregone fact she'd have to leave. There was no way Lancaster was going to take her grandfather's money and not report back to him. She'd had eight years of freedom, she would never go back.

But, damn, she had been happy here. She'd made friends, made a contribution to the school. She didn't want to start over somewhere else. And especially not with Jake Lancaster hot on her tail.

But she'd do it. She'd do anything to keep out of the old man's clutches.

And next time she'd hide her tracks even better--so he'd never find her!

"You've put on some weight since the last time I saw you, princess," he said, "It looks good."

"I was seventeen," she said, her hands growing cold. Thunder stood on alert beside her left knee, growling softly in the back of his throat, his lips lifted over gleaming strong teeth. His eyes never left Jake. One word and he'd attack. Kassie was halfway tempted to utter the command, just to get rid of the man.

But that could cause even more complications. As long as Jake kept his distance, she'd control her dog. She willed the man to give up and leave. Just turn around to get out of the snow and drive back to town. That would give her the time she needed. An hour or two, that's all the start she'd need.

"I saw you right before you disappeared. At some charity ball. Did you walk away or were you really kidnapped?"

Her eyes widened slightly. "There was no kidnapping." Had her grandfather spread that story around? To cover for any eventualities, like her getting killed before she could be rescued?

"Your grandfather paid a hefty ransom. Had a lot of people looking for you when you weren't returned after the ransom was paid."

She smiled maliciously. "Serves the old bastard right. Someone made hay with my disappearance." She didn't even care who it was. She only hoped they made a fortune and stuck it to the old buzzard.

"You?" Jake shifted his weight and moved forward an inch. The dog on the porch leaned forward, showing more teeth with a deeper growl. Jake took a deep breath and eased back. That answered any question he had about the dog.

"Wasn't me. You must know you can't take me anywhere now. I'm over eighteen this time round, Lancaster, and perfectly content where I am. You'd be guilty of kidnapping if you tried to take me back and I'd scream holy hell the entire way."

A brief smile touched his lips. "I'd bet you would," he murmured. His gaze ran down her trim figure, back to her face, noting the hostility blazing.

"Are you going or should I let Thunder escort you off?" She nodded to the dog.

"Your grandfather just wants to see you. Make sure you're all right," Jake said. His hands were growing cold. Were hers? How good was she with that gun? Even as the thought started, his gaze shifted to the dog. He didn't have a chance with that beast protecting her.

"Come on, princess, let's go back. We can do it easy or hard. But you must know by now I always do what I'm paid to do."

"As long as the money's good. How much this time, Lancaster?"

"Enough. You going to offer me twice as much?"

She smiled grimly, remembering her naivety when she'd tried to bribe him last time. She didn't have any money. Just what she'd squirreled away before she escaped, and what she earned as a teacher. Nothing to compare with Judge Martin Sutherland's millions.

Then she frowned, as something sank in.

"He sent you out eighteen months ago?" she asked, puzzled. She'd been gone for more than eight years.

"He had others looking since the day you were . . .er, disappeared."

"I left a note. I told him I wasn't coming back." Kassie was growing tired of this. She wanted him gone. Wanted things to be as they had been yesterday. She hadn't known Jake Lancaster was hunting her, hadn't known her idyllic life was about to end. Damn that old man in Atlanta anyway.

"He conned you, Lancaster. He's a manipulative autocratic domineering bastard. He wants me because I represent the future of his dynasty. I'm his only son's only offspring. He wants to dictate what I do, whom I marry and where I live. I'm over twenty-one now and I'll determine all that."

Jake knew he wasn't going to get anywhere today. She held all the aces with that shotgun and that dog. He'd back off and come back when she least expected. Once he had her without the gun between them, she'd sing a different tune. And even if she didn't, he'd still take her back, one way or the other.

"It's only for a visit. To prove to the old man you're all right. You can be back in Colorado before school starts," he said.

"No." The answer was as plain as she could make it. Her gaze never wavered from his. She felt like she was on a razor's edge, but refused to let a smidgeon of her guard relax. He was wily, but she'd beat him this time.

Jake nodded, turned to climb back into the rental car he'd picked up at the airport in Denver. Shivering slightly, he started the sedan, flicked the heater to high. God, it was cold! His fingers were stiff.

He'd stay in Winter Creek for the night and get some warmer clothes. He'd also decide how to get around her gun and dog. How to talk some sense into her. Her grandfather had aged dramatically since her disappearance. He wanted to see her, to make sure she was all right. Seeking Jake's help had been his last ditch effort. Jake believed the man thought Kassie had died at the hands of the kidnapers. He had to make her understand it wasn't forever, then she'd agree to go back.

If not, he'd take her any way he could manage.

Turning the rental car around, skidding a little in the drifting snow, he headed back to town. The wipers fought against the swirling flakes. Visibility was limited. Slowly he pulled out onto the graveled road, watching her through the rear view mirror, dog and gun still focused on him until the swirling snow blocked her from view.

He'd thought the hardest part behind him. Finding her had been a bitch. She'd learned a lot in the intervening years about covering her tracks. Now he wondered if the hardest part still lay ahead of him. Dammit, he'd spent enough time on this case. He wanted to get back to Atlanta. It was too cold up here. He'd had enough of that as a boy.

He'd been raised, if you could call it that, only a few hundred miles or so north. And what he remembered the most was the unceasing cold in winter, never enough warmth. Clothes that didn't keep out the chill of the Wyoming blizzards in a shanty shack that leaked icy wind at every corner, cold meals on the table--when there were meals.

First thing he'd done when his old man hit him that last time was head for the south. Not that Atlanta escaped winter's cold, but never as bad as here, and never for as long. He hated the Rockies.

Why had she settled here? Now he had to spend another day in this hellhole of ice and snow and wind. He wasn't dressed for it. The jeans he wore were fine for Atlanta in December. Up here he needed more. A lot more.

Impatiently, he jacked up the car heater. He liked the southern climate, didn't want to be caught in this backwater Colorado town for days on end because of some damned blizzard. Or some damn stubborn heiress.

His car skidded again, and he turned into the slide. Concentrate, he told himself. At this rate, he'd be lucky to make it back to Winter Creek. It was snowing so hard he could scarcely see the tracks he'd left on the road, and the wiper blades only piled it up at the bottom of the sweep, smearing it on the windshield, never clearing it completely.

Another curve. The heavy car skidded as Jake fought to keep on the road. For a moment he thought he'd made it, then the rear wheels lost traction and nothing stopped the slide toward the edge until the car slid over, flipping on the embankment, ending on its right side. Jake swore once as his head slammed against the windshield. Everything went black.

Kassie heard the crash. She remained standing in the doorway, her dog on alert beside her. She watched as the car drove away, listening to the sound fade on the storm's soft sigh. Just as she was about to close the door, she heard it. The sound was muffled because of the snow, but she knew he'd gone off the road. Damn him! She slammed the door.

He'd ruined the setup she'd carefully devised for herself. For the last couple of years she'd felt safe. Had begun to believe in a future. She didn't need this. She stood by the window looking out. He'd be back asking to use the phone to call for a tow. Had he deliberately run into a tree as an excuse? It wouldn't work. She'd call a tow truck for him, but he wasn't getting inside.

As the moments passed, she wondered if he'd been close enough to the Maguire's place to go there to call for help. No, they'd left already for the holidays. They weren't due home until early January. The other neighbors didn't live up here year round, and wouldn't return until spring.

Slowly the minutes ticked by. No tall, snow-covered man stalked out of the blizzard which continued to build in strength. Nothing moved but the swirling snow and the tall lodge pole pines swaying beneath the growing intensity of the wind.

Involuntarily she remembered the light denim jacket he wore, the cotton shirt beneath. Neither were suitable for this weather. Had he flown in from Atlanta that morning?

"If this is a trick, I'll kill him," she muttered, dragging on her jacket. If it wasn't a trick, then he was in serious trouble. He could freeze to death quickly in this weather wearing no more than he had on.

"Come on boy," she called Thunder as she pulled a warm woolen cap on her head and went outside to warm up the SUV. Backing out into the snow, she considered getting the shotgun, but knew she couldn't handle it at close range and didn't dare chance him taking it from her. She'd rely on Thunder for her protection.

Slowly she followed the tracks down the road. They were already filling in. A gust of wind caught the side of her car, rocking the heavy vehicle on its shocks, swirled the snow until she could scarcely see the hood.

Driving slowly it wasn't long before her eyes picked up the plowed snow at the edge of the road. She slowed to peer out the window, spotting the Buick lying on its side against a tall fir at the bottom of a slight ravine.

There was no sign of Jake.

She scanned the area, tense, ready to move at the slightest sign of him. Studying the snow, Kassie saw no footprints. Was he still in the car? Had he been hurt? Or had the snow just filled in his tracks as quickly as he made them?

She couldn't imagine him hurt. Somehow she thought him invincible. From their first meeting when he'd taken her back to her grandfather, he'd seemed like a warrior of old. Strong and true to his liege lord, whatever man paid for his services. She'd only wished he'd been on her side. Maybe things would have turned out differently.

She shook the image. It was long ago. She needed to worry about today. If he was injured, she'd have to get him help. She couldn't let anyone, not even Jake Lancaster, die in a blizzard, no matter how much she hated him.

Setting her flashers, though the chances of anyone coming by were remote, she pushed open her door and stepped out into the blizzard's fury.

"Come on," she said to Thunder. "Heel." He bound beside her as she scrambled down the incline, the snow up to his belly in spots. Sliding and slithering, she made her way cautiously down the hill, watching warily every second. If this were a trick, she wanted to be prepared.

Kassie approached the car, its underbelly already turning white with snow, black where the heat of the engine melted the snowflakes. Nothing moved. She hunched in her warm down jacket, reluctantly taking her hand from the warm pockets to pound on the door. Using the pipes and rods beneath the car as a ladder, she climbed onto the car, sliding on the slick icy coating on the door. Grabbing the handle, she hauled herself up enough to scrape the window clear and peer in.

It seemed like twilight inside the Buick, snow already covering the windows. She could make out Jake, slumped against the far door. Hadn't he enough sense to fasten a seat belt?

Pulling open the door was almost impossible, it was heavy and she had to pull it up, then braced against it to hold it open. The snow on the slick paint gave her no traction. Twice she almost caught her hand in between the door and jam as it slipped and slammed shut. Jake didn't move, lying awkwardly against the far door, eyes closed. She heard his harsh breathing over the rising rush of the wind. Finally Kassie pushed the door wide, braced it with a foot, and leaned into the car.

"Jake?"

"Um." He moaned then opened his eyes, bringing

his hand to his forehead. There was a cut there, blood already seeping down to drop on the glass of the window--the knot from the blow clearly visible.

"Are you all right?" she asked.

"Damn." He closed his eyes, and groaned.

Kassie was getting tired of bracing the door. "This isn't some sort of trick is it?" she asked suspiciously, still not trusting the man an inch.

"If you count a throbbing head, a shoulder that aches like a son of a bitch and being so cold I can hardly think a trick, then yeah, this is a doozy of a trick. Caught you."

"Can you get out?" she asked, louder. She knew he must be freezing in that light jacket. She was growing cold herself and was dressed for this kind of weather. Her jacket was thick, down filled. Her flannel shirt warm and she wore long johns beneath her jeans, with thick woolen socks beneath her hiking boots.

"Yeah, give me a minute."

"You don't have that long. This door is heavy and I can't keep holding it open," she snapped, hoping to hurry him along. She had very little purchase on the car and the snow was coming fast. She didn't know how long she could keep it open before she slid off into the snow bank that was building against the exposed underneath of the car.

Jake opened his eyes and looked around, quickly assessing where he was, what had happened. Without a word he moved around on the seat, turning to look up at her, then raised up on his knees. Reaching in his pocket for a handkerchief to put against his forehead he clenched his teeth against the pain, almost blacking out. He wiped the blood from his eyes, then used both hands to lever himself up and out of the car, standing on the steering wheel to get the last distance needed. Unable to stifle the groan moving caused, he collapsed over the edge and let himself fall into the soft snow.

Two

"Think I cracked a rib or two. Damn snow." He paused a moment then pushed himself up and leaned heavily against the car, breathing hard, fighting the waves of raw pain.

Kassie let the door slam, and hopped down to stand warily a few feet away. She never took her eyes off him.

"Come on. I'll take you home and we'll look at the damage you've done," she said resignedly. She'd have to call for help from the cabin. And figure out a way to get him out of her place so she could implement plans to get away.

"Get my bag. It's in the trunk," he said, still leaning against the car, his eyes closed, his face almost as white as the snow covering his shoulders.

"Even supposing I can get it open the way the car is lying, I don't have the key," she snapped. Who did he think she was, some lackey?

He was silent for a long moment, his eyes narrowed against the pain and the cold from the blowing snow. "In the ignition, I think."

"For heaven's sake, how am I supposed to get them if they're in the ignition?" she asked in exasperation.

Jake eyes opened a slit. Her pale blond hair was covered by a bright red knitted cap, already coated with snow. Her cheeks were rosy with cold and her blue eyes blazed at him as she rested her fists on her hips.

"I'll open the door, you just lean over and get them," he said without moving. It was a hell of a time to wonder if her lips were warm or cold. If she tasted as sweet as she looked.

"Right. In case it skipped by your attention, Mr. Hotshot Cop, it's snowing fit to beat the band out here. I could scarcely climb up and open the door to get you out. Forgive me if I don't think you have the strength to stand, much less climb back up the slippery side of this stupid car and wrench open a heavy door. Forget your bag. You won't be staying long enough to need it."

"I'm not going without it," he said, closing his eyes again. His laptop and spare clip were inside. He wanted them with him.

Damn, his head hurt. And his shoulder. And his left side. Slowly he moved his arm, clenched and unclenched his fists. His hands ached with the cold. Was he a candidate for frostbite on top of everything else?

Forcing his eyes open, Jake pushed himself away from the car and took a step toward her. She jumped back. The dog loped up to stand beside her, his low growl halting Jake as nothing else could.

With an effort, he stopped. "Call off the damned dog. You opened the door once, do it again. I'll hold it open from here while you reach in for the keys."

Kassie stared at him. She had only to turn and run

back up the slope to her car for safety. From the look of him he couldn't follow her three feet, much less make any kind of grab for her. But she remembered last time. Did he still carry handcuffs? She stepped back another step, not willing to take the chance he'd shackle her to him a second time.

Thunder never moved, quivering in attention.

A shudder shook Jake's power frame and she could tell how tightly his jaw was clenched by the flex of his cheek muscles. Even with snow covering him as fast as it coated the car, even with the slow trickle of blood across his forehead, down his cheek, he looked strong, and invincible--like nothing could stand in his way.

Once he set himself upon a task, he completed it. Always. He'd told her that himself.

"No tricks," she said, knowing she was giving in, but something made it inevitable. She couldn't leave him out here to die. And if he wasn't going without his suitcase, she'd have to do something to retrieve it or they'd both be out in the blizzard far too long arguing.

"Look, princess, I'm going to be lucky to make it up to the road. From the looks of that canine killer you have, if I look at you wrong I'll be dog food."

Kassie glanced at Thunder, standing right at her knee, his eyes never leaving Jake, the hair on his shoulders raised, the low rumble coming from his throat.

"All right."

Kassie scrambled up on the car again, slipping and sliding worse than the first time. The door was more difficult to open this time. It froze against the frame and didn't want to budge. Finally she drummed her heels against it before yanking it open, almost slipping over the roof. Jake reached up his left hand and grasped the edge, bracing against it to hold it open long enough for her to reach inside. Warily she watched him, looked at the door. The last thing she needed was for it to drop down on her.

Taking a breath, she leaned over the edge, wiggling in to reach the key. She had to turn it back and forth before she could withdraw it.

Jake clenched his teeth against the pain in his side and the throbbing in his head. He hoped he could hold it open long enough for her to get out. He watched her struggle, his gaze roaming over her body, hidden for the most part by that thick jacket she wore. But the rounded curves of her bottom were clearly defined as she leaned over and it was all he could do to keep his hands on the door and not moved to feel the warmth of her through the snug jeans she wore.

"Nice," he murmured. He was getting light-headed. Especially thinking about Kassie's physical attributes when he was about to freeze to death.

"Huh?" She asked, sliding out, holding up the keys in triumph.

"Your tight little ass--nice," he said as the door slammed shut.

Her head jerked up and outrage filled her eyes as she met his with a startled gasp.

"Don't even think it," she warned as heat kicked in through her belly.

"Honey, you can't stop a man from thinking what he's going to be thinking. Especially waving that nice derriere in the air right in front of him," Jake said, giving her a slow, pain-laced smile as he slid down to sit on the snow-covered ground.

"I don't believe this," she stated. "I'm just a case to you, remember? You don't care about me as a person at all. Don't start having any kind of thoughts about changing that." She dangled the keys before him. "If you want your suitcase, you get it. I'm at the top of the hill." And she turned and marched up the snowy embankment, slipping and falling twice before gaining the top. She yanked open the door of the Bronco and climbed in, calling Thunder to hop up beside her. Let Jake Lancaster prove how macho he was and get himself up alone.

The minutes ticked by. Kassie grew impatient. Where was he? Snow fell heavily, piling up on the truck. She'd have to brush off the windows before she could drive. Where was he?

Impatient, she opened the door and called his name. Nothing.

Concerned despite her distrust of the man, Kassie climbed back out into the storm and went to the edge of the road. She spotted him half way up the hill, lying down, his duffel bag a few feet below him. Had he hurt himself again? She slid down to him. He was unconscious.

"Arrgg," she screamed. "How did I get into this? You weigh a ton," she murmured, trying to lift him. She succeeded in getting his head in her lap. Gently she wiped the snow from his face. He felt icy cold. The blood from the cut had stopped bleeding, but whether from natural coagulation or from freezing, she wasn't sure.

"Don't you die on me, Jake Lancaster," she said, shaking his shoulder. Talk about complications. She did not need the media flocking around because a man froze to death practically in her backyard!

"Wake up, do you hear?"

"Cold," he muttered. "So cold."

"I know. Just a few more steps to the car. It's warm there. We'll be home in a jiffy. Come on, we don't have time for this, get up!" She urged him up and he half crawled, half stumbled his way back up the hill. When they reached the road, Kassie slipped her arm around his waist to give him support. She felt the hard metal bulge at the small of his back and stumbled. Gingerly she withdrew a gun and handcuffs. He didn't even notice, his attention focused solely on reaching the car.

She stuffed them in her pockets and opened the passenger door. Helping Jake in, she looked at Thunder. "Guard," she instructed. Then she went back down the hill one last time to get his damned duffel bag, wondering if he'd appreciate any of the trouble she was going to for him.

She didn't want anything to do with the man, but she couldn't let her worst enemy die in a blizzard.

And that is what Jake was, or the next best thing to it. She'd best remember that.

She drove to the Johnson's driveway, turned around and carefully retraced her route home. The snow was several inches deep on the road and treacherous. She skidded, even driving slowly in four-wheel drive. The distance seemed endless. The wiper blades smeared the windows. The heater blew lukewarm air. Finally she saw her roof. They'd made it. Pulling close to the porch, she thankfully cut the engine. Turning to look at her uninvited guest, Kassie saw he was unconscious again. The cut on his forehead steadily dripped blood and it was smeared all over the front of his jacket.

Was he seriously hurt? Would he need medical attention? She could not drive all the way into town without killing them both. The storm was growing worse.

Climbing down from the high SUV, she opened the door to the cabin and went back to get him. He appeared groggy, but opened his eyes to mere slits. Stumbling together, they made it up the three steps and into her living room.

The roaring fire had burned down to embers yet the room seemed like heaven after the biting cold of the outdoors. Kassie slammed the door behind them keeping in what warmth remained. Jake had to weigh a hundred pounds more than she did and every one of them leaned on her.

It took a bit of doing, but Kassie was able to get him as far as the guest bedroom and thankfully released him to sink on the unmade twin bed. As a token to normalcy, Kassie had purchased the bed a few months ago, though she had no friends nor family that she expected to use it.

He lay supine, breathing hoarsely, the blood now oozing back to soak into his dark hair. She stared at him in anger. If he hadn't tried to find her, he wouldn't be here now. What was she going to do with him?

"Damn you, Lancaster. Why didn't you stay in Atlanta?" she muttered under her breath as she stomped off, shrugging out of the down coat and draping it over a chair in passing. She knew he wouldn't be going anywhere tonight. Not the way the snow was coming down. His injuries didn't look life-threatening, though she couldn't be sure of that, she was no doctor.

Hiding the shotgun, to make sure he didn't use it against her, she then gathered a washrag, bowel, towel, and her first-aid kit. She stormed back to the guest bedroom, anger hovering at a near boil. She ought to turn him out into the cold and let him fend for himself. He had brought her five years of purgatory and now was back trying for more. It was not going to happen!

He hadn't moved.

Sighing, she placed the bowl on the floor and knelt beside the bed. Soaking the rag, she blotted the blood from his wound. He groaned softly and shifted his head slightly as if to escape her ministering. She ignored him and continued sponging his face and hair until the rag came away clean. The bleeding slowed. Gently she pushed the skin together and placed a gauze pad across it, anchoring it in place with adhesive tape. Then she sat back on her heels and studied him.

"Jake?" Gently she shook his shoulder.

"What?" His eyes stayed shut.

"Are you awake?"

"How could anyone sleep through your nursing? I felt my head would come off," he said in a surly voice laced with pain.

"Look at me so I can see if you have a concussion."

One eye slit open and he stared at her in disgust.

"Practicing medicine now, princess?"

"Common sense. I'll call my doctor in a minute, but want to see if your eyes are focusing equally."

Both lids raised and he stared at her, his dark blue eyes deep and mysterious as he gazed into hers. Intense intelligence beamed from both eyes, no signs of unawareness or concussion evident.

"Want to check the rest of me so you can give the doctor a full report?" he asked his gaze indolently running over her, skimming her breasts concealed in the flannel shirt, dropping to her waist-- as far as he could see from his position.

"A quick rundown will do," she said, hoping the tremor in her voice wasn't transmitted. She wanted to slap his face for his obnoxious leering look, but wouldn't give him the satisfaction of knowing he'd disturbed her.

Disturbed her? He had ignited a flame deep within her she'd never felt before. She flushed, felt the flickers of heat like ribbons of fire throughout her entire body. She didn't need this. She wanted nothing to do with the man except to get him out of her life and move on.

Next time she'd hide so deep her grandfather's hired hunter would never find her, she swore.

"I banged my shoulder against the door, whacked my knee against something. And it's hard to breathe. Must have bruised some ribs," he cataloged for her.

"Or cracked them. Why weren't you wearing a seat belt?"

"Is that your school teacher voice?" he asked, hoping to divert her from the reason he'd not fastened the belt. He'd been taken aback at her holding the gun on him, at the dog by her side. And mad as hell he'd been caught off guard. Obviously all the updated information about Miss Sarah Caroline Sutherland had not been conveyed in the last report.

When had she learned to use a shotgun? She was a missing debutante, not Annie Oakley.

She frowned and rose, picking up the dirty water.

"We'll see what the doctor says."

Jake ached in every bone in his body. He lay still, watching her walk from the room. Now what? He'd be willing to bet his fee for this assignment that she was already planning to run. He couldn't very well go after her in his condition.

Man, he hated snow and mountains and godforsaken towns in the middle of nowhere.

He gritted his teeth and sat up. The room swayed a moment, then stilled. It was already dark, but he could see from the light spilling in from the open door. Slowly he stood, his body screaming in protest. Once on his feet, he felt better. An aspirin or two and he'd be fine.

"Kassie?" he called.

"I'm still on the phone."

A moment later Kassie appeared in the doorway, her eyes watchful and her manner tense. Seeing Jake on his feet, walking toward her she wanted to push him down on the bed and run. Escape while she still had the chance, before the hunter regained his strength and trapped her. But she forced herself to stand still and watch warily as he stepped closer.

"Playing Florence Nightingale changes nothing," he said.

"I never thought it did. As soon as the roads are clear, you're leaving. So will I, now that you've discovered where I live. But we are not leaving together."

"He just wants to know you're all right," Jake said gently, as if trying to coax a shy woodland creature.

"Like hell he does. You don't know him very well if you believe that," she said. She wasn't fooled. And she wouldn't be coaxed back. If she ever went, it would be tied and unconscious. But she vowed he would not take her any way at all.

"Give him a chance," Jake urged.

"Call him and let him know you've seen me and I'm fine. That should reassure him," she said daringly. "But don't give my location away. He'll be all over me like flies on road kill. Sorry, Lancaster, you're either as big a bastard as he is, or as big a fool as I'd be to believe you."

The doctor came on the line and she watched Jake as she spoke with the physician. She stepped back as if the unwanted pull of attraction would be lessened by distance.

"Okay, I'll do that," she said. Clicking off the phone she glared at Jake. "The doctor says to watch you for concussion, and bring you in as soon as the roads are passable. Aspirin or something for pain."

Jake nodded.

"It's late, do you want something to eat?" she asked. If she fed him, maybe he'd go to sleep and she'd have some time alone to plan. The weather screwed everything up. Every second he was here brought danger closer. Had he tracked her down alone? Or had her grandfather set others after her as well?

"Sounds good."

She spun around, glad to leave the tense situation and flee for the safety of her kitchen. Thunder patiently stuck by her. Thank God for her dog. He offered the only safety margin she had.

Jake followed. She snapped on the bright kitchen light and pulled a plate of leftover roast beef from the refrigerator. In only moments she set a thick sandwich down beside him. Two minutes later a large glass of milk joined the plate. She glared at him as if defying him to comment on the beverage.

Jake murmured a quick thanks and picked up the sandwich.

She eased toward the door.

"Stay and talk," he said. Ordered.

She watched him warily. "We have nothing to talk about. Your position is clear. So is mine."

"We can talk about other things." Jake didn't want her going into the other room. He wanted to keep an eye on her, though how he thought he could do anything in his condition if she chose to defy him he didn't know. But he was uneasy with her out of sight. It had taken him a long time to find her. He was not going to lose her now.

"The doctor says he thinks your ribs sound cracked, but I bow to your superior knowledge if you think they're only bruised. If we were closer to a hospital, he'd x-ray them. But the storm's worse and I can't drive you there. And you're not critical enough for an ambulance to be dispatched in this weather. So it's bed rest only." She didn't move from the door.

"Thanks for taking me in."

"I'd do it for anyone," she said. The anger still simmered just below the surface--and the fear. She had to escape. And she couldn't even think straight with him hovering over her every second.

"Even though you didn't want to?"

"Yes. I'm not a murderer and leaving anyone out in weather like this–especially when they are injured and inappropriately dressed–would be tantamount to murder."

"And you're familiar with that, right?" he asked.

"What do you mean?"

"Didn't you believe someone was out to kill you?"

Kassie tightened her lips. She still believed her life would be in danger if she ever returned to Georgia. Jake Lancaster hadn't believed her then. He certainly wouldn't believe her now.

"Just recover enough to get out," she said.

"When I go, you'll go with me."

"When pigs fly. Finish eating and go to bed. No one's going anywhere tonight. It's a real billy blue blazing blizzard out there. I doubt either of us will be leaving for a few days, dammit." She turned and stalked into the living room, her dog padding patiently beside her.

Jake awoke, instantly alert. For a long moment he lay perfectly still, assessing where he was, trying to determine what had wakened him. His chest hurt when he breathed. His head pounded like drums in mismatched tempo. When he slowly eased to his side, his eyes wide, a sharp burst of pain stabbed his shoulder. Gritting his teeth, he sat up. It felt more comfortable than lying down. He checked his watch, a few hours until dawn. Was it still storming? Straining, he heard nothing. Only silence.

He found his shirt and jeans on the chair across the room and drew them on, leaving both unfastened. He clenched his jaw against the pain in his ribs and shoulder. He hadn't hurt like this in years. Just proved he was getting too damn old for field work. Ten years ago he would have bounced back instantly.

Gingerly he rotated his shoulder, trying to loosen the muscles, trying to ease the fierce ache. Slowly, silently he approached the door, eased it open until he could gaze out into the living room of the small cabin. It was deserted. A dim glow outlined the coals in the wood burning stove. The door to the other bedroom was shut tight.

He searched for the dog. Had Kassie taken him in her room for protection? Checking the time again, he crossed silently to the kitchen, his bare feet making no sound on the cool wooden floor.

Seeing the phone on the wall, he reached for it. His cell was probably still in the rental car. He dialed quickly. Patience was a trait necessary for his kind of work. Everything would turn out just the way he wanted if he were only patient enough. But he wished John would answer--

"Yeah, this better be good," a grumpy voice growled into the receiver.

"It's Jake."

"Damn, do you know what time it is? It's six in the morning! Where the hell are you, anyway?"

"Listen, I don't have long. What did you find out?"

"With the info you gave, we hacked into the school computers. She's been there four years. Not much else. We can't get into her bank account, so don't know how her finances are. Other than electricity and phone, she must pay cash for everything, no trace of credit. Can't believe she's working as a teacher with all her money."

"Yeah, weird."

"So when will y'all be back here?" John asked. All trace of sleep fled from his voice as he clicked into action.

"There's a slight complication. Winter's biggest blizzard is dumping all the snow in hell. I wrecked my car yesterday trying to get back to town from her place." No need to tell John he'd been heading back alone. He peered out the window, but the light from the kitchen reflected on the glass, making it impossible to see anything but his own reflection. "I don't know how long it's going to snow, but it may be a day or two before we can get out."

"At least you've made contact. How is she?"

"Fine. Doesn't want to come back."

"So slap the cuffs on her like last time and get back here. You've finished that assignment. All hell broke loose two days ago. Haley got off."

"Damn!"

"Yeah, well, it gets worse. Someone bombed the office last night. Blew half the floor away. And it's raining buckets, so most of what's left is in shambles."

Jake tensed up. "Anyone hurt?"

"Naw, happened after Brianna left for home. But word on the street is that Haley's gunning for you. Better get back here and start a backfire."

"Go find him. I can't do anything before sunup. Then we may have to tramp out." If he could walk that far. Time enough in the morning to worry about that.

"So it's just you and the fugitive, huh?"

"I'll be along as soon as we can get out." Jake stared at his reflection, his partner words reminding him of the last time he'd brought Kassie home. How frightened she'd been, how defeated. He hadn't liked it then and he didn't like thinking about it now. Funny how the memory had lingered all these years.

"Jake, you still there?"

"Yeah. Can't use the cuffs this time. I think they're buried in about four feet of snow. In fact, if she really puts up a fuss, there's not much else I can do but let the old man know she's safe and where's she living. Beyond that--she's over twenty-one and on her own. As she keeps reminding me." Jake said without a speck of amusement.

"I'm sure he's going to love hearing that. He doesn't pay us the big bucks to find out where she's living. Bring her in, pal. We can use the money. In the meantime, I told him yesterday that you found her and y'all will be back before long."

Jake knew they could use the money. But they could also manage without it. They had several firms under contract for security work. Others lined up. This job for Judge Sutherland was more to help out an early client than a necessity.

But Jake prided himself on finishing what he started. And so far he'd seen nothing about this assignment to change his mind.

"I'll see you in a couple of days," Jake said heavily. The last time he'd taken Kassie Sutherland home, he'd needed the money. The circumstances were different this time. Maybe he should forget trying to get her back. Let the judge come to see her. John had told the old man she was all right. Maybe that would be enough.

He started the coffee. He wouldn't sleep any more tonight, though it was far too early to be up. Obviously his body was still operating on East Coast time.

As he watched the dark brew drip into the carafe, he wondered at the family relationship between Kassie and her grandfather. The old man seemed genuinely worried and anxious to have her back in the fold. She seemed equally determined to stay away.

No love loss there. She hadn't even let her grandfather know she was safe in more than eight years. Or asked after him when Jake said he was here on his behalf.

Jake had no family. His mother had died when he was small, his grandparents before that. He'd been raised by a father who had no business having children. At seventeen he'd had enough of his father's fists. He'd left Wyoming determined to get as far away from everything he knew as he could.

When finding work proved impossible, he joined the army. After he got out, he trained as a cop. Until he'd quit to start his own security business with John Ashbury, he'd been a good cop. Now he took pride in his own firm. The two of them had built it from the ground up. And they always delivered.

He had no family and no fond memories of growing up.

But Kassie was different. She had a loving grandfather who was worried sick about her. A grieving aunt. Other relatives whom he'd seen from time to time at the charity events they so lavishly supported.

Kassie had thrown away all that attention and care in a tantrum. It was a waste, and Jake hated waste.

The closed door in the far living room wall cracked open and then widened. Thunder padded out, his golden eyes immediately seeing Jake, his gaze never wavered.

Kassie followed, pulling on a warm robe. Her hair was tousled and one cheek was pink as if she'd been laying on it. She looked warm, sleepy--and desirable.

Jake felt a sudden tightening low in his belly as he stared at her. For an instant, he forgot she was a case. She looked beautiful. Her blond hair drew his gaze like a magnet. Was it as soft as it looked? It still had that silky shimmering shine.

For a moment he let himself imagine her in bed. She'd be warm and cozy beneath the quilts, her skin satiny soft. He'd like to skim his fingertips over her, imprinting the feel of her on his every cell. Seeming untouched and ethereal gliding across the floor, she widened her eyes when she saw him staring at her.

He'd kept tabs on her after he'd returned her to her grandfather. She'd gone off to finishing school in Switzerland for a number of years. Then returned to Atlanta. Before she'd disappeared, she'd attended several charity events. He had finagled his way in to one just to see her. She had appeared regal and elegant in her fancy designer dresses with sparkling jewels at her throat and wrist.

But there had been an air of aloofness, of distance. The ice princess.

Now she looked warm and cuddly and infinitely more appealing.

"Is something wrong?" she asked, moving from the living room into the doorway of the kitchen, keeping a safe distance between them.

"I couldn't sleep, so I fixed some coffee." He nodded to the coffee maker, his eyes skimming over her.

She was wearing woolen socks, a flannel nightie peeked beneath the quilted robe. The voluptuous folds hid her figure, but he knew she was slender. Not teenage skinny like the first time he'd seen her, but slender, feminine, yet curved in all the right places.

"That's bound to help you back to sleep," she said, her eyes trailing down his open shirt, the unzipped jeans.

She jerked her head up and walked around the center table to the coffee maker. Color stained her cheeks.

Jake felt her look like a hot poker. How could

anyone be cold with her watching them the way she'd been studying him? The heat that pooled in his belly moved lower and he zipped up his jeans before his reaction to her wide-eye stare embarrassed them both. Dammit, he was on an assignment and that did not include fantasizing about his subject.

"Was it warm enough in your room?" she asked. "I switched on the base heater."

"Yes. Warmer than out here, but the coffee'll take care of that," he said, leaving his shirt unbuttoned. Almost daring her to look at him again.

"How do you feel?" she asked politely.

"Head aches, my ribs are giving me fits and my shoulder feels like a field kicker used it for practice," he said casually as if of no importance. "But I'll live long enough to take you back to Atlanta."

Three

Kassie looked up and met his gaze, saw the fire banked in his eyes.

"I can get you some more aspirin," she said, ignoring his provocative statement.

Kassie turned and hurried back to her room, desperate for a moment to collect herself. Her reaction had shocked her. She yearned to reach out and touch that hot skin, trace those muscles to learn their shape, their feel. She'd wanted to brush through the light covering hair on his chest to see if it felt crisp and crinkly, or soft and silky.

His comment cut off that desire as quickly as a hot knife cut through butter.

Was she losing her mind? The man was her enemy, she must never forget that!

Belting her robe more securely, Kassie snatched up a bottle of aspirin. Returning in only a minute, she concentrated on keeping her expression passive. She dare not give any hint of the tangled desires she'd felt only moments earlier. No telling what the aggravating man would say. Or try to use it against her.

She approached him warily, bottle opened, ready to

spill the tablets into his hand. He held up his right hand and as she shook the tablets out, his left hand grabbed her wrist.

Caught!

Her eyes darted to his, locked. Heart beating rapidly, she considered her options. She'd been a fool lulled into a kind of security. His implacable gaze convinced her he was still dangerous--injured or not. Could she yank free?

"Where are the handcuffs when you need them?" Jake asked whimsically, his thumb caressing the soft skin of her wrist.

Kassie felt her pulse kick in to high gear. She knew he'd felt it as well when he stilled his thumb on the beating point. His eyes darkened and he gazed down into her eyes. She did nothing to camouflage her emotions. Furious, she wanted to rail against him, against fate, for again putting her in such an untenable position.

"Let me go." Her voice soft, she didn't move, didn't try to pull her hand free, just glared at him. One word to her dog, and she'd have nothing to worry about. Had he forgotten Thunder?

He held her gaze far longer that she liked. Could he see every emotion that tumbled around inside her head? She clung to her anger, determined that was the only emotion she'd allow him to see.

"Point made," he said and gently opened his fingers to release her.

Kassie refused to turn and flee, though that was her immediate impulse.

"I'll get you some water." She walked to the sink, her arm burning from his touch. Her heart raced in reaction. If he'd had his handcuffs, she knew he'd have used them in that moment. Bound her to him physically so they'd never be apart until they reached Georgia. Thank God she'd hidden them along with his gun and her shotgun.

"You don't need to wait on me," he said gruffly.

"You don't know where the glasses are." Her answer was reasonable, but her fingers trembled slightly when she took the tumbler down--filled it with water. She felt his gaze on hers, assessing, calculating. Turning, she offered it to him, watching warily.

Holding her gaze with his, he tossed the tablets in his mouth and reached for the glass. Covering her hand with his, he tilted the glass against his mouth, drawing her hand with it.

Kassie was shocked to her toes at the rampant sensations that flooded. His hand burned hot and hard holding hers against the glass. Tingling electricity zinged up her arm. His dark eyes refused to release her. She feared he'd see the strange reaction she experienced. Every ounce of reason in her screamed she should hate this man.

But her body betrayed her.

For years after her enforced return she had thought of him, planned dire punishments for his part in her pain. When she could think straight, that was. When her mind wasn't fuzzy from the drugs. When she wasn't watching her back to keep from being killed.

Now his touch had her imagining warm nights, hot

kisses and raw sex.

She flushed, praying he couldn't read her mind. He was dangerous to her safety, to her freedom, to her very sanity. She needed to run as fast as she could in the opposite direction.

Instead, she found herself fighting a strange longing to step closer, touch his cheek, feel that thick hair that curved against his collar, run her hands over his chest to feel the heat given off by that tantalizing bronze skin.

"Thank you," he murmured, his voice low, seductive.

Kassie blinked, afraid to speak lest he detect the tenuous control she held.

"Did I thank you for getting me out of the car?" he said slowly, drawing her nearer still until Kassie felt the heat she'd only imagined from his chest through the thickness of her gown and robe.

"No need," she said, knowing she should pull back, but her limbs felt peculiarly heavy.

Thunder growled. The spell was broken. She yanked her wrist from his grasp and stepped away. Tightening her sash, she backed to the kitchen door.

"It is still the middle of the night, and I need sleep even if you don't. Thunder, heel."

Head held high, she marched to her room, fearful every step Jake would try to stop her. But she reached the bedroom without incident. Closing the door, she snicked the lock. She leaned her forehead against the cool wood. How safe was she really? One good kick and the flimsy lock would shatter. But for a moment, she had the illusion.

It was after nine when Kassie dressed and ventured out into the main part of her home. Jake stood by the front window, studying the landscape.

She shrugged on her jacket and pulled on a woolen hat. Taking Thunder out first thing was safer than staying inside with the man. But it was freezing cold, continued to snow, and she couldn't wait until they returned inside.

"It looks as if it will snow all day. When the storm lifts, we head back to Atlanta, but it won't be today," he said without turning when she entered the main room after Thunder's walk.

"No, Jake, when the storm lifts, you can hike back to whatever rock you crawled out from under and leave me alone. I'm not going anywhere with you." She dried her dog, and shook her jacket free of snow before hanging it up.

"We'll see. Did you forget I'm bigger and stronger?" he asked.

"Oh, you're going to try a repeat of last time? Snap those handcuffs on me and drag me back. Not this time."

He turned and looked at her. The seconds ticked by. "I don't have my handcuffs, where are they?"

"Gone. Too bad, now you'll have to stay away from me."

"Ah, but that's something I can't do." He reached out and caught her wrist again.

"Let me go." Kassie refused to tug her arm free.

"Say please." He tightened his grip relentlessly until he could see the discomfort reflected in her face--pain she tried desperately to hide.

"Please," she bit out, glaring at him.

He opened his hand releasing her, feeling like the bastard she called him. What had he proved?

Her hand swung in an arc and landed satisfactorily on his cheek. The sound was like a gunshot. Thunder came tearing into the room, headed straight for Jake.

He backed to the wall, his head feeling like a ton of bricks had landed on him. The pain was almost unbearable.

"Call the dog off." He could barely get the words out. His vision was growing a little black around the edges.

"Keep you damn hands to yourself in future, is that clear?" She stayed the German Shepard with a hand motion. The dog's steady gaze never left Jake, the growling deep in his throat rumbled throughout the room.

"Clear."

She took in a deep breath and turned to her dog, gently stroking the thick fur on his head.

"Where's my gun?" Jake asked.

"So you can shoot me?"

"We're not playing games here, Kassie. My job is to get you back to Atlanta," Jake said, visibly easing away from the wall as the threat from the dog receded. He needed to sit down. Not that he wanted her to see he wasn't in top form, but if he didn't sit soon, he feared he'd crumble to the floor. His head was throbbing.

"For the last time, I'm not going back to Atlanta with you or anyone else. You can forget about using your gun or those blasted handcuffs, I tossed them in the snow when I found them on you," she lied. "Go hunt for them if you want them so badly," she snapped.

His lips tightened but he said nothing.

Kassie walked into the kitchen and poured herself a mug of coffee. She rummaged in the bread box and drew out a partially used loaf. Tossing two pieces into her toaster, she heard him enter behind her. She could see his reflection in the shiny side of the toaster. He leaned against the door jamb, watching her.

"Why did you come here, Jake?" she asked, turning, leaning against the counter. "Was it some ego trip? You're the only one good enough to find me? Or is it the money? You did it for the money before, didn't you? You're a cop, but on your off hours you do work for hire?"

"Was a cop."

Kassie shivered slightly, afraid of him, afraid of what he represented. Could she win? She was older, had the law on her side this time. There was nothing he could do to take her back legally.

But would that stop him? Or would the lure of the money her grandfather had promised override any scruples on his part?

"Was a cop?"

"I quit almost five years ago. Started a security business."

"So what kind of security work was it tracking me down?"

"It isn't. Part of the appeal of the assignment was the challenge. Your grandfather approached me when you first disappeared after the ransom had been paid but you weren't returned. I didn't take it on then. Eighteen months ago he asked again. By then, you'd been gone for so long, it was a challenge." He ambled over to the sink and poured a cup of coffee.

The toaster popped up. Kassie took the brown slices and caught up her cup, moving to the table.

Jake remained where he was, took a sip of the hot brew. "Plus I can always use the money."

"Everything comes back to money. And my grandfather knows that. He's a master at getting people to do what he wants, and he can afford to buy whatever it is he wants," she said bitterly, looking at her coffee, avoiding Jake. It hurt somehow to know that he was after her only because of the money. Not because of some strong conviction, or a desire to right a wrong.

It was strange, she didn't know him, except from their brief encounter years ago. Yet he was unlike any man she'd met since then. She felt hurt he'd come after her only for the money. Maybe she'd thought he would have higher ideals, being a cop and all.

"Of course you did it for the money before," she said quietly. Why should she be surprised?

"I needed money before and moonlighted wherever I could. The amount your grandfather paid went a long way."

"And you need it again now."

"For different reasons, but it'll come in handy." Jake watched her, trying to figure out what the various expressions chasing across her face meant. He had never been good with women. Witness Tricia. Now he wanted to know what was churning around in Kassie's pretty blond head.

Kassie. He liked the name--it was sassy and lively and seemed suited to the bright teenager he'd busted at that department store in Philly so long ago.

"It wasn't easy to trace you," Jake said.

"You're a bounty hunter. Selling people's lives for money." She rose and looked at him seeing a hard man threatening her very life solely for money. "I think you're disgusting," she said clearly and stormed back to her room, leaving the uneaten toast on the table.

The door slammed in the quiet cabin and Jake heard its echo over and over. Along with her words.

Bounty hunter.

Was that what he'd become? Selling someone just to line his own pockets? Not a pretty picture. He studied the dark brew in his cup as if seeking the answer.

He was doing a job for an old business acquaintance. A man who had never done him anything but good. A man who was worried about his only granddaughter and wanted to know she was all right. An old man who didn't have the luxury of time to wait for her to return on her own.

Kassie was furious with herself. She needed to remain cool and collected if she was to get out of this mess. She had no time to feel anything for the blasted man in the next room except anger. Time was growing short. She had to disappear again!

Could she do it so Jake Lancaster couldn't find her? She had taken such pains before, and thought she'd been successful, until yesterday. Would she be able to evade him in the future? Especially with him only hours behind her, instead of years?

Or was there another way? Some way to get her grandfather off the idea of controlling her life. Get him to cut his losses and let her go.

She knew that was impossible. For the eleven years she'd lived under his control. He'd dictated her every move, tried to dictate her every thought.

Before that he'd tried to run her father's life. She could still remember the angry words, the bitter recriminations.

If she had enough money she'd offer Jake twice what her grandfather had to forget he'd found her. Bribe him to report back that he'd lost the trail. But she didn't have any money, not of the magnitude to combat her grandfather's wealth.

To go back would only endanger her own life. She'd been kept drugged and complacent for years. Twice she'd escaped death by sheer dumb luck. Now that she was on her own, she knew she couldn't allow a third chance.

She knew the Honorable Judge Martin Sutherland himself wanted her dead.

Jake sat at the table until his coffee grew cold. Taking one final swallow, he rose and dumped the rest in the sink. His headache had eased some, due to the aspirin and caffeine no doubt. It was growing cooler and he went back to the living room, adding another log to the fire. Sitting gingerly, he leaned against the sofa cushions, idly staring into the flames as he reviewed what he knew about Sarah Caroline Sutherland and her grandfather, Judge Martin Sutherland.

He knew better than to let any kind of personal feelings enter into his job. It weakened him, threw the outcome into jeopardy. But without warning, Kassie's image danced on the flames.

When he'd gripped her wrist, he'd noticed the softness. He'd been trying to make a point and had ignored the silky texture of her skin. He could have crushed her wrist. She was delicate and delightfully feminine. Though she probably wouldn't see it that way.

Her lips were naturally rosy. Though she had a tart tongue, witness her scathing insults, he bet she'd be sweet to kiss.

Damn, she was a case, not a potential date.

He smiled mirthlessly. He'd never see her as a date, and she'd probably laugh her head off. He'd seen her several times when she'd first returned from school in Europe, before she'd disappeared.

Each time she'd appeared cold and distant. Granted, the few charity affairs he'd attended probably hadn't been her forte. They weren't the parties and country club dances he knew she was used to, so maybe that caused her to look distant--regal.

The dresses she'd worn would have cost him a month's pay. And her jewelry was always different, sapphires to go with a blue dress, diamonds with a black one; rubies with a white one.

Living the way she had over the last eight years must have been a huge come down. The clothes he'd seen her in yesterday didn't remotely resemble designer fashions. Jeans that looked faded, flannel shirts, scruffy hiking boots didn't fit his image of Miss Sarah Caroline Sutherland of Atlanta, Georgia.

She said it had been her choice. There was something more to it than a spoiled rich girl flaunting her grandfather's wishes. There had to be. Her whole life style had changed. Drastically.

Something didn't fit.

Was there anything to her claim that someone wanted her dead?

He doubted it. But maybe he'd listen to her next time she mentioned it. Ask a few questions. Find out what made her tick, why the dramatic change in life style. She'd lived this way too long for it to be a whim.

Why was she fighting so hard against going back? She just had to meet the old man, let him see she was fine, and return to Winter Creek.

Kassie probably dramatized everything. Maybe something she'd heard as a child had her thinking of plots and intrigue that simply didn't exist. Talking through it as an adult, could he make her see the impossibility? If he did, would it make it easier to take her back to Atlanta?

After a polite Christmas visit with her relatives, she could return to Colorado and continue the new life she'd made for herself.

Hell, was he playing crusader now? Trying to mend the rift in their family?

For a moment he let his mind wander as far as imagining her changing her mind about him. Could she understand his position twelve years ago? She'd been underage, a runaway. He'd simply returned her to her family before she could come to a bad end.

Now, however, she was right, times had changed. Circumstances changed. He did not have a legal leg to stand on.

Drifting off to sleep, Jake wondered what her grandfather would say if he had a clue to the thoughts that jumbled in Jake's mind. How he'd like to see Kassie lying on a sheepskin rug before a roaring fire, the golden flames sending soft illumination on her skin, her eyes soft and hot, her mouth moving against his.

Judge Sutherland probably would commit murder-- his.

Kassie leaned against the windowsill, keeping a wary eye on Jake. How long would he sleep? She'd been surprised to find him on the sofa when she left her room. Yet where else could he go—except back to bed. The doctor said he should rest.

The snow had fallen steadily during the night. Over a foot piled up on the railing of the porch, mounded over the tarp-covered wood piles. Angling her face against the cold glass, she saw the driveway had disappeared. She couldn't begin to tell where the road lay. The skies were low, overcast and gray. How much longer was it going to snow? The report yesterday had only mentioned last night. She'd listen to the radio later, see if how bad the storm was and when it was predicted to stop.

Not that the weather listened to the weathermen. It did whatever it wished up here and Kassie often thought the weathermen only played catch up. If it was wet out, they announced rain. If it was sunny, they announced fair skies.

Her stomach grumbled. She was hungry. Anger had eased, and now she wanted to eat. As she prepared sandwiches, she went over her plans. She'd slip out just before dark. She didn't want to try the road to the highway at night. Even though the snow was deep, she knew the SUV could plow through it. Once on the highway, she'd head north. Maybe this time she'd try California. There were a lot of people in that state, surely she could hide there.

She had money hidden around the house. Most of it had been there since she moved in. Always ready to move at a second's notice, she couldn't depend upon banks. Her check was deposited, she kept enough in her account to pay her bills, start a small savings account. The rest of her money she withdrew and kept in cash at home. A good thing.

She'd gather it all up today, from the various hiding places, and see how much she had. It would be all she could count on until she could get another job.

And she couldn't chance a teaching position again. It had been difficult enough getting this one. Schools would be the first place Jake looked when he came after her again.

She sighed. She loved teaching. Would she ever be able to go back to it? Only when the man who wanted her dead was no longer in the picture.

She sat at the table and ate her sandwich, wondering what food she could take with her. If she carried enough, she wouldn't leave a trail in restaurants.

Jake stirred. She could see him from where she sat.

"I made lunch, there are sandwiches here if you want something to eat." She waited for him to slowly rise, then walk into the kitchen. Several sandwiches were piled high on a plate. Two place settings sat opposite each other on the table. Grateful she'd already eaten, she watched him warily. She'd be safe with the table between them.

"Still snowing," Jake said, sitting opposite her.

"Could for days. I'll listen to the radio later and see what the forecast is."

"While we wait we have a chance to get to know each other better," he said.

Kassie frowned. "I have no intention of knowing you any better. I know all I want to about you. What I want is you out of my life once and for all!"

She already knew enough to find him dangerous. She knew what he wanted and how hard it would be to outwit him.

And she knew she was attracted to him. Not that she would ever admit that to him or anyone else.

Anyway, it was sheer physical proximity. She couldn't really want to get entangled with the man.

"You can fill me in on what you did after school in

Switzerland," he said.

She looked up, surprised. "How did you know about that?"

"I called a week or so after I took you back and was told you'd left for school in Switzerland."

She stared at him, confused. "Why did you call?"

"To see how you were."

"If you had cared at all, you wouldn't have taken me back."

"Sarah, you were a minor, a missing person whose family wanted her back. I was just . . . "

"Playing bounty hunter!"

He reached across the table so fast she didn't see it coming. His hand gripped her arm and he half-pulled her from her seat, leaning across the table to meet his face, inches from hers. The anger in his eyes and the tightness in his jaw frightened her.

Thunder had wandered into the other room and couldn't see the danger she was in. She opened her mouth to call him, but Jake spoke first, his voice low and hard.

"I'm no bounty hunter. I was a cop bringing back a minor who'd run away from home."

"I turned eighteen three weeks later, but had no hope of escaping by then. I was incarcerated in that Swiss school for four years. I had a body guard with me constantly. Every damn place I went. Then when I returned to Atlanta, I had bars on my windows, was totally restricted in what I could do, whom I could see. My body guard was there for companionship, so my grandfather told everybody. But she was nothing but a damned jailor. That's how I was--damn you! You sent me back to that hell and I hate you."

Thunder must have heard the anger in her voice because he bounded into the room, lunging for Jake.

He crashed into him, knocking him from the table. Jake fell against the wall, his face a grimace of pain.

"No, Thunder, no! Guard! " Kassie's arm felt jerked from its socket by the abrupt pull when Jake was knocked back.

"Are you all right?" she asked, rubbing her arm.

"Am I still alive? God that hurt." He pushed up against the wall and glared at the dog.

"You can't manhandle me," she said angrily, reaching out to touch Thunder.

"You made me mad," he murmured, taking a slow breath, testing how far he could inhale before the pain became too much. "But I'm not going to hurt you. Tell your dog that."

"He didn't know. It looked as if you were hurting me." Frowning, Kassie realized that she believed him. He might try to take her back to Atlanta by whatever means he had to use, but he'd never physically hurt her. "You can't keep touching me like you have the right to do so whenever you wish," she said, straightening the chair. "Sit down and I'll get you some more coffee."

Jake used the chair to pull himself up, sitting as he caught his breath.

His hand shot out again, catching her upper arm, more gently this time, but holding her in place nonetheless.

"Maybe I want to touch you whenever I can," he

said slowly, still breathing carefully.

"I'm not some plaything you can paw anytime you like."

He chuckled then grimaced at the sharp pain. "Funny, I used to think of you as an ice queen. You always looked so uppity at those charity functions I'd see you at. But you have a temper."

"I hated those events!" she said passionately. "I was forced to go. I was forced to do a lot of things I didn't want. Being drugged does that to you."

He didn't reply but searched her face as if he could divine the truth. She had emotional problems. The papers he'd been given when he found her the first time attested to them. Was she still loony?

She slammed his coffee cup down before him and snatched his empty plate. Washing the dishes, she tried to ignore him. She had to collect her money and pack. She dare not let him suspect.

Tonight. She'd make her break tonight no matter what the weather.

Four

By the time the cabin was warm and the kitchen cleaned, the snow had stopped. The day remained overcast. Kassie studied the snow for a while and then put on her parka.

"Where are you going?" Jake asked from the sofa in front of the fireplace.

"Out to clear off the walk way. If it snows even more, it's harder to clear than if I keep it off as much as possible as it piles up," she said, pulling on her knit hat and taking her gloves off the mantel where they'd been drying.

"I'll go out with you," he said, rising. From the grimace he made, Kassie knew he was still in pain.

"If you like," she said, knowing he didn't have the proper cloths for Colorado winters. He wouldn't stay out long.

Stepping outside, Thunder raced by her and jumped into the snow. He dashed over to a tree, lifted his leg while he surveyed the white yard. Kassie made sure she didn't get separated from her dog. He was the only thing that kept her safe from Jake.

"Damn, it's cold out," Jake said a moment later.

She moved to the far side of the porch to retrieve the snow shovel.

"That's the way it is in winter," she said. She clumped down the shallow stairs and turned to clear the snow. He stood near the closed front door as if dying to return to the warmth of the house, but not willing to leave her. Wise move. Given the chance, she'd take off in a heartbeat–if she could dig out her car and once she had her cash.

For now she was doing what she'd done many times over the last few winters, clearing snow from her steps and walk way and then her car. She liked the crisp clean air, the hush as the snow muffled sounds. Only the scrape of the shovel against the steps sounded in the quiet.

Jake didn't move, watched her as she worked. She did her best to ignore him. She could wait him out. She had the proper cold weather clothing, and the exercise kept her warm. Once he gave up and went back inside, she'd clear the car and start it, maybe turn it around so it was heading out.

Smiling at the thought of his reaction when she started the motor she turned away lest he suspect.

Thunder ran over to her and barked.

"Okay, okay, okay," she said, jamming the shovel in a snow bank. She reached out for some snow, made a ball and lobbed it into pristine snow. He was off like a shot, stopping short, looking around, sniffing the snow. She laughed. It was a favorite game of theirs. He gave up and ran back to her, barking again.

Over and over they played. Thunder never got

tired.

But Jake did.

She looked up at one point and he was gone. Back inside to the warmth. She petted the dog and resumed clearing the walkway. Assessing the woodpile lining the front of the house, she debated bringing more from the back. Not that she'd need it. She'd be gone long before she could use up what was on the porch.

She opened the car and got her brush. The snow was light enough to brush off the car. Before long it was clear, though a few drifting flakes suggested more snow was due.

She fished out her keys and climbed inside. The roar of the engine had Jake bursting from the cabin at a full run.

She sat in the front seat, door still open and gunned the engine twice more as he reached her and grabbed hold of the door. He'd shed the jacket he wore and was in just his shirt.

"What the hell?" he said.

"Just making sure the car starts," she said innocently, trying to contain her laughter.

He caught his breath, leaning over a little, holding his left side.

Thunder approached the car, his eyes watching Jake.

"Call off your dog, I'm not doing anything," he said.

"Nor am I. Get away from the car."

"Turn it off and give me the keys."

"When pigs fly," she said, challenging him. "Make

one move to get them and I'll kick you in the ribs."

He stared at her for a moment. "You would, too, wouldn't you?" he said softly.

"Believe it." She clung to the steering wheel, hoping he wouldn't try it. She had a spare set he didn't know about, but she was not giving up this set easily.

He stepped back and turned to the house, glancing at the dog. "Go if you're going. I'll just come after you again."

She knew it to be true. She had to be even more clever next time to escape and remain unfound. Glancing at the road, she could scarcely see where the edge was. Everything looked flat, white. She still planned to leave today, but not yet. It would be easier to disappear once it grew dark than with the entire day ahead.

Jake stood by the window watching her. His head was pounding and his side burned from his mad dash outside. She sat in the car, the door still open, letting it idle. Thunder sank down near the car on the snow and sniffed the air.

Damn, he hated winter. If she tried to escape, he might not be able to stop her. He would follow, but it would be a pain in the ass. He wanted to get back home. Turn her over to her grandfather and wipe any perceived debt off the books.

Once again he wondered about Sarah Caroline Sutherland. Why throw off the family ties and hole up in a remote Colorado town, teaching children in a private school of all things. It didn't make sense.

He discounted her tale of drugs and coercion.

She'd been diagnosed with a mental disorder when he'd gone after her before. Was it schizophrenia that had people seeing conspiracies everywhere? Could she function normally for a while, fooling everyone around her? Observing her at the café yesterday, he saw she was well liked by those at her table. In every respect he would have said she was normal. But maybe prescription drugs kept her on an even keel. Her grandfather's concern was more than her not keeping in touch. He probably worried about her mental health as well.

Kassie shut off the car and got out, shutting the door. The dog rose and wagged his tail as he went over to her. Jake hadn't counted on the dog. And she was extremely careful not to put herself out of sight of the German Shepard. He couldn't leave the dog behind. It wouldn't last long without food and water, and the cold would invade the cabin once the fires stopped. Another complication to deal with.

He turned and went to sit down before she could enter. Maybe he needed to back off a bit, lull her into complacency and then take charge. They weren't going anywhere any time soon, not with the snow piled up on the road, and more likely to come down.

It felt good to sit. He shifted slightly to ease the ache in his side.

She and the dog came in, bringing in a burst of cold air. Thunder shook off the clinging snow and padded over in front of the fire, sinking down with a sigh. He rested his head on his paws, his eyes tracking Kassie as she shed her jacket and put the gloves back on the mantel to dry.

"It looks like more snow," she said, shaking the knit hat and positioning it to dry.

"It snows in Atlanta, but nothing like this," he commented.

She shrugged. "I think it's beautiful."

He didn't respond. Snow was best viewed on a post card as far as he was concerned.

"Do you ski?" she asked.

"I have done some, but not recently. I don't like snow."

She grinned. "I love it. And love to ski. I plan to do some during vacation–" She stopped abruptly as the reality of her vacation took over.

Jake felt a hint of remorse that he was wrecking the plans she'd made. He liked seeing her excited smile when she started her comment. Now anger clouded her face. He could almost read the thoughts in her mind–when would she get a chance to ski again?

The phone in the kitchen rang.

He rose and headed that way, but Kassie was faster.

"Hello?"

"Is Jake there?"

She frowned. "Who wants to know?" she said, stepping away from Jake when he stopped next to her.

"John."

She glared at her unwanted guest. "Did you give out this number?" she asked.

"Is it John?"

She nodded.

"He has caller ID and I called him earlier."

She thrust the phone at him. "Don't tell him where we are."

Jake didn't tell her he'd done so days before. Not that it mattered. Did she think her grandfather was going to make a flying visit to Colorado?

"Jake," he said taking the phone.

"Couple of things you should know," John said without preamble. "The grandfather's sending an escort to Colorado. Should be there later today."

"Damn. Did he say why?"

"Nope, just said he was sending reinforcements."

"I don't need any help."

"I've been watching the weather there. They're still landing planes in Denver, but it'll take whoever a long time to get through the roads the way they're clogged with snow and abandoned cars and trucks."

"Any update on the roads to Wyoming? We could get out through Cheyenne," Jake said.

"Where's your laptop?"

"Buried in a couple of feet of snow near the place I crashed the car. Don't know if there's any WiFi here anyway. Check flights for me."

"Checking. In the meantime, Brianna said the main computer is gone."

"Blown up in the explosion?"

"Nope, apparently nothing resembling that was in the debris. She's been working with police and fire in cataloging what was damaged, what's missing. The files were all pulled from the cabinet and spread out like confetti and with the water, they are pretty much completely trashed. At least she backs up everything on a cloud."

"You think Haley?"

"I do. Anything on there that might compromise where you are?"

"Only my itinerary. I had Brianna make all the reservations. If he's behind the theft and bombing, he'll already know I'm here. Same difficulty for him and his men as for the others. This is one hellacious storm."

"Roads aren't looking good. But the worst of the storm is south of Cheyenne. If you can get through it looks as if the airport's open and you can get a flight out."

Jake glanced at Kassie. She leaned against the counter, watching him like a hawk.

"I'll check in later and let you know what's up," Jake said. "I need warmer clothes before we get too far. It's freezing here."

"I know how much you like cold weather," John said with a laugh.

"All assignments in the future have to be south of Mexico."

"Talk to you soon." John hung up.

Jake replaced the receiver and looked at Kassie.

"We need to leave. Any extra winter clothing?"

"Nothing that will fit you. And I told you, I'm not going anywhere with you."

"Well, you may not have a choice. There could be...complications."

"Like?" she asked suspiciously.

"Like your grandfather has sent someone else as an escort, and there may be a guy hunting me."

"You told my grandfather where I was?" She almost yelled the question. Thunder came running into the kitchen at her tone.

"He paid me. I give periodic updates." Jake didn't need to justify his actions. But the fear and anger that warred in her expression made him a touch defensive.

"And who's hunting you and why would they come all the way to Colorado rather than just wait until you're home?" she asked, putting out a hand to ruffle the fur on Thunder's neck.

"Long story. Probably going to do exactly that. So the sooner I get you to your grandfather, the sooner you'll be out of that."

Kassie took a deep breath and glared at him. "Remember I have Thunder and a shotgun and I wouldn't hesitate a moment to turn them both loose on you."

Jake almost smiled. If he closed his eyes, he'd have a better time believing the pretty woman in front of him could act in such a violent manner. But right now she reminded him of a kitten, all claws and hisses that he could scoop up in one hand and sooth.

Only he didn't doubt her for a moment.

"I'll take you up on lunch," he said.

The words were barely out of his mouth when the light in the kitchen went out.

Kassie looked up. "Power's out. I expected it. Happens all the time. Actually with the snow as thick as it is, I'm more surprised it stayed on this long."

"So what do you do?"

"Wait until it comes back on."

"No generator?"

"I have a small one in the pump house to power the pump for the well, and I can run an extension cord to power the refrigerator. But in weather like this, I just take the refrigerator stuff and put it in the snow." She nodded toward the back door.

"You're on a well?" Jake asked.

"You don't think they have city water out this far, do you?"

Another aspect he hadn't considered. This woman was not some pampered princess of a wealthy man. The conflict from the picture he had based on how her relatives viewed her and the reality was amazing.

"Are you on meds?" he asked.

She looked up and frowned.

"What are you talking about?"

"Whatever mental disorder you have, are you taking medication for it?"

"I have no mental disorder," she snapped. "Never have. Those papers were faked. Worked for you, didn't they? Made sure grandfather got his way. Things are different this time. I have friends who have known me for several years now. Others who knew me then—and are independent of any control of Judge Sutherland. You don't have a leg to stand on and if you take me across any state line, I'll scream kidnapping so loud and clear nothing will keep you out of jail."

Thunder came to his feet, facing Jake.

"I'm not kidnapping you," he said patiently.

"I'm not going willingly."

"Impasse."

"As soon as the storm is over, you can hike out and get back to wherever you came from," she said.

"Unless it warms up considerably, I'd freeze before I got to the main road."

"You should have thought about that before you left home," she said.

Kassie headed for her room, calling her dog with her. She closed and locked the door. Taking a book from the shelf near her bed, she lay down, pulling a quilt over her legs. Trying to read proved futile. She couldn't let go of the pressing urge to get away.

If her grandfather sent someone else to help Jake, it would be twice as hard to avoid being taken against her will. It was probably a doctor or someone the judge had convinced she'd need sedation. Then they could do anything with her.

She kicked off the quilt and rose. Taking a backpack, she reached in her top drawer and pulled out the money she'd taken from her hiding places while Jake slept. She spread it out on the bottom of the backpack. She had several thousand dollars saved. It would have to tide her over who knew how long before she could get another job.

Packing some wool socks, thermals, another shirt and some basic necessities, she glanced around the room. She loved this cabin. She had picked each piece of furniture and decoration from the second hand shops in the area. It was the first place she furnished totally the way she wanted. She resented the need to leave. Resented the fact her father's father would not leave her alone.

She didn't know what else to do but run.

Otherwise she faced a life of being drugged until one day the end came.

"Not if I can help it," she murmured. The pack was heavy, but not more than she could handle. Once she had her winter coat, hat and gloves on, she'd be good to go. She took Jake's gun from the hiding place in the floor and stuffed it down in the pack. The shotgun wouldn't fit, but she could carry the pistol. The only thing to do was evade Jake long enough to make her escape. He already showed he was quick when he heard the car start–even injured as he was.

Next time he'd do more to keep her from leaving. Only next time, she'd have the car doors shut and locked and gun her way out and if he got in the way, too bad for him. She wouldn't stop for anything!

When Thunder had to go out, she opened her door and closed it quickly. She'd put the backpack in the closet, but no sense in letting Jake think he could look into her room whenever he wanted.

He was lying on the sofa, asleep.

She stared down at him for a moment, struck by his hard look even in sleep. Nothing seemed to soften that angular face. His stubborn jaw only reiterated what she knew about him. He was tenacious, dogged and determined. Not a bad trait if he were only on her side.

She slipped on her coat and went out with Thunder. He did his business and they played a little in the snow. It was already getting dark. No more snow had fallen, but the skies stayed overcast. There was a light breeze, but nothing like the wind that could kick up.

For a moment she gazed at the pretty setting. She loved living here. Would she find another place she'd love as much?

Thunder stood on alert, his ears up, looking toward the main road. Could he hear the snow plows? Were they already nearby, or still concentrating on the town streets first?

It didn't matter. Her car could handle the snow if it didn't get any deeper. She was only waiting for the right moment.

As the afternoon waned, it grew dark in the cabin. The lack of electricity was annoying as the overcast sky didn't give much light so reading was difficult. Even the phone was dead. With no television or other means of entertainment, Kassie grew more and more angry that Jake was invading her space.

He read one of her magazines, then tossed it to the coffee table. The noise startled her. Thunder raised his head and looked at Jake, then toward the door. Rising, he walked over and scratched once.

"I'll take him out," Jake offered.

"No thanks." Kassie put on her parka. "Come on, boy, let's go outside for a little while."

Thunder wagged his tail, his ears alert as he faced the door. Once open, he took off, heading for the nearest tree.

The air was cold and damp. Snow covered all the trees. Even though she'd cleared her car, additional snow had covered it with a light coating. The wipers would clear the windows, but she walked over to brush some of it off the back. A glance at the house showed

Jake standing by the window watching her.

She could run the car again just to worry him, she thought mischievously. The keys were in her pocket. She opened the door and started the engine. Sure enough the front door opened. But instead of rushing to the SUV like last time, he merely stood there watching her.

She debated calling Thunder and closing the door on them just to show Jake she could. But the thought wasn't that appealing. Sighing, Kassie wished she could turn back the clock a couple of days to have never been found.

After a moment, she turned off the engine.

Thunder raised his head, his gaze focused down the road. He growled and walked closer to the car.

"What's up, boy?" she asked, getting out and shutting the door. She ran her hand along his back where the hair near his neck was raised. She looked down the same direction. Only endless whiteness met her gaze. "Come on, Thunder, let's go back inside."

She shivered, wanting the safety of her house. The afternoon waning light was depressing. Soon they'd have to light oil lamps for light. And it'd be soup and bread for dinner. The burners on the gas stove would work, she could light them with a match. Too bad the oven had an electric igniter.

They headed inside, but once the door was closed, Thunder lay down beside it, his ears still upright.

"What does he hear?" Jake asked, moving to look out the window again.

"I don't know. But he's making me antsy."

"He's been trained well."

"Yeah. K-9 class, but flunked out."

Jake looked at her. "How do K-9s flunk out?"

"He chases cats. Nothing they could do would break him of that."

Jake smiled.

Kassie stared at him, taken aback by how much the smile changed his look. He caught her gaze and raised an eyebrow in silent question.

Flustered, she looked away. "I'll fix soup for dinner."

"Sounds fine to—"

Thunder surged to his feet, growling, his stance pointing to the door.

"What in the world?"

Jake went to the window again. Then before Kassie followed him to look out, he dropped to the floor just as the window shattered.

"Get down," he hissed.

Thunder barked, lunging against the door, again and again.

"What is it?" Kassie stooped down. "Thunder, down!"

The dog ignored her, barking and lunging again and again as if trying to break down the door.

Another shot rang out. The upper window shattered. Then bullets came through the wooden door.

"Thunder, come," Kassie screamed. The dog reluctantly turned and headed for her, looking back at the door. She scooted back, toward her bedroom as the window in the dining area shattered. Covering her ears, she could scarcely breathe for fear.

Jake rose in a crouch and ran across the room to her. "Where's your shot gun?" he asked.

Another round of bullets came through the door.

"Who's out there?" she cried. She turned to him and hit his arm. "You did this. You told my grandfather, didn't you? Damn you! Now he's trying to finish what he started before. I could shoot you myself."

"It's not your grandfather," he said.

"Then who would come here and shoot up my house?"

"It's me they're after. And they won't stop until they get what they came for."

Thunder barked again. Bullets slammed into the house, the log siding, the door.

"Where's the shotgun?" he demanded.

"I'll get it." She crawled across her bedroom and retrieved the shotgun from the recessed hiding place in the floor. Dragging it behind her, she scooted to the closet, pulled out her backpack and crawled back to Jake.

He snatched the gun from her and headed for the living room windows.

"They'll shoot you there," she said, feeling the cold swirl around the room with the windows gone. The heat from the stove was dissipating faster than she imagined.

"Not here. You have a stack of wood under the window that'll stop any bullets." He peered over the sill, pumped the shells into position and half rose as he fired two shots almost as one. He sank down and looked at her.

"Any way out of here?"

"The back door if there's no one out there."

"My guess is these guys haven't done any recon yet. They thought to catch us unaware. We need to leave."

"You'll freeze to death before we can get very far. Next time you come to Colorado, you should dress more appropriately."

He almost laughed. "We're about to be killed and you're talking about next time I come here? If I get out of this I'm never coming back—especially in winter!"

He rose and fired off two shots.

"Did you hit anything?" she asked, still clutching Thunder. The big dog faced the door, growling deep in his throat.

"No, mainly I'm trying to buy us some time and keep them wondering. How many more shells do you have?"

She went back to the hiding place and pulled out the box. She didn't have a lot of ammo, using most of it for practice time and again. She wanted to be prepared, but nothing prepared her for this.

She slid the box across the room; staying where she was, fear flooding her with adrenalin.

"If we can make it to the Maguire's place, you could get something from Mac's closet to keep warm," she said, trying desperately to consider their best escape route. Everything was at least knee deep with snow. Could Jake make it to the Maguires?

"Who are the Maguires?" he asked, peering over the window sill. A round of gun fire had him ducking immediately.

"My next door neighbors, down the road a bit.

They're gone for the holidays. I have a key to their house. But that would mean leaving the car. We'd have to walk out in all this snow, leaving tracks all the way. I don't want their house all shot up."

"They have any guns?"

"Maybe. Yes, I'm sure. He's a hunter."

Jake shot off two more shots and nodded.

"Get as much warm clothes on as you can. We'll leave in five minutes. Will the dog stay with us or head for these guys once he's in the open?"

"He'll stay with me." Kassie hoped that was true. If Thunder took off after whoever was shooting, she knew they'd have no compunction in killing her dog.

She crawled to her room and pulled on a sweater and a thick sweatshirt, then back to the living room to yank her coat down from the hook and put it on.

"My hat's on the mantel," she said.

"Leave it. If we make it to your neighbor's, you can find one there," he said.

In only seconds she was by the back door, Thunder's leash was attached to his collar.

"Ready," she said, just as another barrage of bullets sprayed the house.

"Listen, this is the drill. You leave. Keep as hidden as you can in case they can see from the front. I'll follow in a few minutes following your trail and doing my best to wipe it out behind me," Jake said, leaning against the wall, reloading the shotgun.

"How will you do that?" she asked, gripping Thunder's leash, her heart pounding.

"I'll find an evergreen branch and drag it behind

me. Not perfect, but the light's going fast. The longer they delay in finding we've left, the more chance we have of it being too dark for them to track us."

"And of you missing my tracks."

He looked at her. "End of your problems if that happens."

She glared back. "I wouldn't wish a frozen death on anyone–even you!"

"Go, Kassie. Get away."

She nodded and dragged her backpack on. She urged Thunder to the kitchen, crawling on her hands and knees. When they reached the door, she cracked it opened and spoke to her dog. He quivered with excitement. "No, Thunder, heel. Just heel. We aren't going after bad guys."

She was outside in a heartbeat, expecting each second to feel a bullet tear into her. But it was silent. Then she heard the shotgun and took off for the trees behind her house. Once far enough away from her house not to be seen, she and the dog turned to head for the Maguires. It was hard going in the deep snow and with the waning light, she had no depth perception and couldn't judge how the terrain unfolded. Twice she fell to her knees, her jeans soon coated in snow. Thunder jumped and plowed through the snow at her side.

She heard gun fire again, then the shot gun, but it was distant. She should be near the neighbor's house. Turning she tried to find it, but it was darker than before and there would be no lights to guide her there.

Another five minutes and Kassie began to worry she'd overshot the house. What if she missed it? Got lost in this forest and wandered around until she succumbed to the cold? If Jake couldn't follow but the men with the guns could, they'd succeed in killing them both.

Jake said they were after him, but how had they found him? He had to be wrong, these assassins were from her grandfather, she knew it once she learned Jake had told the old man where she was. Once Jake had reported in, her grandfather's influence was wide enough to send men after her to make sure she didn't get back to Atlanta. He could disavow any knowledge of her in Colorado. No one would ever tie him to her death.

Thunder pulled on the leash tugging her to the right. She looked in the direction he was pulling. Was that the house? She followed and soon saw the Maguire's house, covered in snow. Circling to the front, she fished her keys out of her pocket and let the two of them in.

The house was cold. They would have left the pipes drained and turned things off. Knowing there was no electricity, Kassie didn't even try to turn on the lights. But when she bumped into a chair, she knew she had to find some kind of light. Feeling her way into the kitchen, she began opening drawers, feeling in each one to see if they contained candles. In the third one she found candles and matches. The candle didn't give a lot of light, but at least she could see where she was going.

Heading for the bedroom, she ignored the feeling of trespassing. She knew Max and Marge would want to do whatever they could to help her. She rummaged around in the closet, finding little that would help Jake.

Of course, winter coats would be in the closet by the front door. She opened a couple of drawers, finding thick woolen socks. Another drawer revealed thick sweaters. Grabbing a couple, she headed back to the front of the house. The closet near the front door had a worn winter jacket that would be big on Jake, but warm. She found knit hats, gloves, scarfs. Pulling them all out, she made a pile by the front door.

Kassie went to the bathroom, not knowing when she'd be able to use facilities again. Then washed up with the wipes she knew the Maguires kept in the cupboard beneath the sink. Going back to the kitchen, she checked each cupboard, pulling out as much food as she thought would travel and putting everything in one of the reusable bags Marge kept by the back door.

Finally satisfied she'd purloined all that would help them, Kassie went back to the living room and sat in one of the chairs, pulling a nearby afghan over her legs. She blew out the candle and sat in the dark. Waiting.

Thinking.

She had to get away, but she couldn't leave Jake. Not until they were both safely away. She knew what lengths her own family would go to. Jake didn't believe it, but she was living proof. Once he was outfitted against the cold, they could head for town. She has several friends there she could call on. Help was only a few hours away.

It was time to make plans. Where would she go next? She hated to leave the friends she'd made these last years, but this place was no longer safe.

She regretted leaving her students behind as well. It

had been an act of faith from Sophie Montgomery to let her use her transcript from their school in Switzerland to let Kassie pretend to be her. She couldn't involve Sophie again. How she'd get another job was beyond her right now. But then, anything but getting away from the men with guns would have to wait until she was safe.

Thunder growled. Kassie wished she'd taken the gun from the backpack. It was by the door with the rest of the things.

Then she heard a quiet knock.

"Kassie, it's Jake, let me in."

She went to the door and opened it. Thunder wagged his tail and whined.

"Quiet," she commanded as Jake staggered in.

"Damnation it's cold!" he said.

She shut the door, feeling the coldness radiating from him.

"I have a candle," she said, lighting it. "There're wool socks in that pile, sweaters and Max's old winter jacket. He's lots bigger than you are around the middle, so you ought to be able to wear the sweaters and the jacket. Wool socks will keep your feet warm even if they get wet."

"The little naturalist." he commented, sitting on the floor and pulling off his wet shoes and socks. In less than three minutes, he had changed socks, pulled on two sweaters and the jacket. She handed him a knit cap and pulled one over her own head. The gloves were next.

"Do you need a potty break?" she asked.

"What?"

"If we're heading out, you might—"

"I'm not one of your students. If I need a potty break, I'll find a tree."

"And freeze your—"

"Okay, point taken. Where is it?"

She handed him the candle. "Down that hall," she pointed.

When he returned, she had her backpack on and was holding the bag of food.

He emptied the pockets of his jean jacket of the shells he'd brought, putting them in the pockets of the heavy jacket. Picking up the shotgun he nodded. "Know where we're going?" he asked.

"Town. I have friends there who can help. If only to lend you a car so you can leave."

"You think we can just walk into town from here? It must be fifteen miles."

"You want to go back to the cabin and get the car?" she asked.

He blew out the candle. "No. They could be on this doorstep any minute. Though I think they won't be traveling very fast in the dark. But a couple of flashlights would be all they need to follow. Or, once they figure out where we're going, they could wait in town."

"Then we'll go to Stephan's. I'm not sure I can find it through the woods, but if we can walk near the road, I can."

"Who's Stephen?"

"The guy who got me Thunder. He's a retired cop. You two should have lots to talk about."

"Lead on."

Five

Kassie took a breath when they opened the door. The house was cold, but it was even colder outside. Worried about the men after them, she headed down the stairs and turned for the concealing trees.

"It'll be easier walking on the road," he said. "We can hear them if they come, and see their lights most likely. They aren't going to be driving in the dark without lights. And if we walk in the tire tracks, it'll be easier than pushing through the snow drifts. Plus we'll know where we're going since you know the way by road and not, I'm thinking, through the woods."

She thought about it for a moment. It made sense and she knew they'd hear a car before it could illuminate them in headlights.

"Okay." Anything to make it easier to walk in the snow. It was hard going and she knew it was several miles to Stephan's house.

They trudged along silently in the tracks the gunmen had made. She wished they had a flashlight, but any light would give them away. Still, with no light, it was hard to stay in the tracks. Only when stepping in deeper snow did she realize she was out of the tracks.

The backpack grew heavier with each step. She shifted the bag of food to her other hand.

"Give me that," Jake said.

How had he even seen it in the dark, she wondered, glad to hand it over. Maybe he'd offer to carry the backpack, too. Then she remembered the money and pistol in it and decided no matter what, she kept that with her.

They trudged for what seemed like hours. When they reached the main road, the snow plow had been through once. Snow still covered the asphalt, but at least it was minimal and the berms on the side helped differentiate the road from the forest and made it much easier walking. When they reached it, Kassie hesitated only a moment then turned away from town.

"How far?" Jake asked.

"I don't know. It takes me about five minutes in the car. So maybe four or five miles. His road's probably not plowed either." That would make it harder for the men after them to find. But harder for Jake and her to navigate.

They heard the car several moments later and, reacting as one, jumped over the berm and lay down in the snow. Thunder lay beside Kassie, nosing her as she shushed him and held her breath.

The car went by slowly, heading toward town. Not the men from the cabin, then.

"We should have flagged them down," she said softly as the noise from the engine gradually faded.

"We don't know who it is."

"The car was heading toward town."

"So, they could have taken off when I did. Not following me, but sweeping the area to find us. Driving out before I reached your neighbor's house, and then slowly retracing the area."

"I still think it would have been better to flag them down."

"Know of many people who will stop for two strangers and a dog after dark?" he asked.

"Actually, lots of folks around here would," she said softly. "I wouldn't like to view life like you do."

"Keeps me alive."

"Barely if those guys back at the cabin are anything to go by. Your logic's faulty," she added.

"Why's that?"

"If they're after you, why shoot at me? Why not wait until you're on your own and move in?"

"What if they think you're my girlfriend? More damage that way, hurt someone I care about before I get killed."

"Ummph. If they only knew," she muttered.

"Let's go."

She could hear the amusement in his tone. Glad someone found something humorous in the night.

Brushing off the snow, they climbed the berm and returned to the road and continued. Kassie was tired, cold and hungry. She tried to see her watch, but the battery was weak and the light faint. It didn't matter what time it was, she was hungry.

"I wish we'd had dinner before they arrived," she grumbled.

"What's in the bag?"

"There're some granola bars. I'll take one or two. I'm hungry."

He stopped and fished out a couple, handing one to her and opening one for himself.

Thunder sat on her foot and she broke off a piece of hers to give to him. "He's using up more energy than we are," she said. "At least we have clothes to help keep the warmth in."

"With that fur coat he has, he's fine."

"There's some bottled water in the pack, too. I want one," she said after she finished the bar.

He stopped again and offered one to her. "At this rate it'll be dawn before we get there."

"Be glad I know some place to go. You'd still be back at the cabin now if not for me," she said, unable to feel very charitable toward Jake. He'd disrupted her life completely in the last two days. "Or floundering around in the woods trying to evade those guys and not having a clue where you were."

The snow created a hush unlike any other. The only sounds were the occasional clump as a branch released the snow, and the crunch of their footsteps on the powder-covered road. Kassie hoped she could spot Stephan's turn off when they reached it. It wouldn't be plowed, and it was all they could do to keep on the road with the help of the berms. How she'd know where to turn off was beyond her.

They heard another car. This one was behind them. Again they jumped off the road and lay in the snow. The lights soon swept above them. The snow glittered in the headlights and Kassie felt it was so bright whoever was driving was sure to see them. She closed her eyes tightly as if that would conceal her.

The car continued on its way, however, without even pausing. Soon the light vanished and the noise of the engine faded.

"Wish we had a flashlight," she said again, brushing off the snow.

"Too dangerous."

"Being with you is too dangerous," she mumbled.

"Once I get you home, you don't ever have to see me again."

"I'm not going back to Atlanta!" she said. He knew that. He just didn't believe it. What would it take to get it through his thick head!

As they continued, Jake began to feel lightheaded. His ribs burned like a brand. His head throbbed and his shoulder couldn't take the weight of the bag, so he kept it in his right hand which was starting to cramp from the weight. He hoped he could go the distance. She'd said it was several miles. They were not exactly breaking world records with their speed, and if she found the road they needed in the darkness, he'd start believing in miracles.

He also wished they could use flashlights. Or if he were wishing, he'd wish he'd never heard of Haley, or been part of the team to take him down.

The gunmen were after him. He was sorry Kassie got involved. Had he known the extent of Haley's reach, he never would have had their secretary handle travel arrangements. But he'd thought the man safely in jail.

Now he had killers on his trail, and a job to complete with a woman who would fight him every step of the way.

He didn't want to go there. Not unlike last time,

Not that he believed her story that she was drugged.

Yet, it would explain her behavior the few times he saw her in the years before she disappeared. If she were drugged, emotions would be suppressed and she would appear aloof and distant. Zoned out.

A niggling suspicious thought came to mind. Surely her grandfather was only looking after her best interests. He was a well-known philanthropist. Well respected in the community. He couldn't be trying to kill his granddaughter no matter what crazy notion Kassie entertained.

But what if he were?

It didn't matter. He'd accepted a job and he'd carry it through. Hell, he could stay with Kassie when she met the old man and then escort her back to the airport after the visit if that's what she wanted. She could trust him to keep her safe. And hold the judge to the agreement— bring back his granddaughter. There was nothing that said she had to remain in Atlanta.

Once he delivered her, that job was done. He could then take on whatever he wished—including bodyguard to Sara Sutherland or Kassie Montgomery or whatever name she wanted to use.

It had to be close to midnight when Thunder whined again and bumped against Kassie's knee.

"What?" she asked. She was cold and tired and her legs felt like wet noodles. All she could do is trudge along, blind and cold. One foot in front of the other. She wasn't sure hell was hot, it could be miserably cold which would be an awful way to live.

He whined again and walked in front of her, tugging on the leash, heading for the berm.

"Do you have to go potty?" she asked, loosening up the leash. He pulled ahead.

"Good grief, just go on the road. You don't need a tree," she grumbled.

Thunder jumped the berm and tugged on the leash, barking twice.

"Shhhh," she said.

"What's he doing?" Jake asked, retracing the steps he'd taken ahead of her.

"I think he needs a tree."

"I could use one myself, but not to pee on, just to lean on and rest a while."

"It's freezing out here, we're not sitting under some tree like it's a summer evening," she said, climbing the slight berm and following Thunder. The dog bypassed the first tree and continued on.

"Wait, can this be the road to Stephan's place?" she asked as Thunder continued up the wide swath cut through the trees. "Oh, I hope so. I'm so tired and cold." It was hard not to whine and just drop in her tracks, but she pushed through the drifts, struggling onward. Dogged determination kept all complaints bottled up. She'd not give way to venting where Jake could hear.

It wasn't easy to walk in the deeper snow, and before long Kassie knew her feet were there, but couldn't feel them. She felt Jake keeping pace with her one step behind. If she stopped suddenly, he'd plow into her.

Then she saw the lights through the trees. A house. Not Stephan's, his was farther along, but maybe Thunder had recognized the road and was leading her to Stephan's

Fifteen minutes later she stumbled up the stairs to the familiar wide deck and knocked on the door.

Jake scanned the area, hoping they were far enough away from the men after them that they'd never be found. Not that they could stay here long. The sooner he got back to Atlanta, the sooner he could work out a plan to get Haley for good.

The door opened a crack. "Who the hell is it?"

"Hi Stephen, it's me, Kassie. I need your help."

The door opened wide. "Come in. What are you doing out here this time of night? Hey, Thunder, how are you, boy?"

Once inside, Kassie sank down onto the floor, leaning against the wall. "I may never move," she said, letting the warmth of the house seep into her.

"Who's this?" Stephen asked studying Jake when he stepped in behind her.

"It's a long story. Stephen, meet Jake. Jake, this is our host for as long as he'll let us stay, Stephen."

Jake nodded. He swayed.

"You okay man?" Stephen asked, reaching out a hand.

Jake looked at the older man. For a moment his vision blurred. The ex-cop was not quite as tall as he was. But he still looked fit and in fighting shape. Couldn't have been retired too long, was his thought before he swayed again.

"Hey. Come over here and sit down."

He went to the sofa using the last bit of energy he had. Collapsing down, he leaned his head back. "She's right, I may never move again either." He closed his eyes. The last thing he remembered was Stephen asking what the hell was going on.

Morning brought clear skies and sunshine sparkling brilliantly on the snow. The room was full of light when Jake opened his eyes. He winced at the brightness and closed them again. Gradually he became aware of voices in the next room. Kassie and Stephen, he thought. He had to get up. If they were up and raring to go, no telling what Kassie told the man about him. The sooner they got on the road, the better.

He moved to sit up and groaned as his ribs protested with a pain so sharp he gasped for breath. Thunder padded over and stuck his nose in Jake's face.

"Back off," he said.

The dog sat and looked at him, his tail wagging on the wooden floor.

"Awake?" Kassie asked from the doorway. "We've already eaten breakfast, but Stephen kept a plate warm for you." She frowned. "Are you okay?"

"I will be. Give me a couple of minutes."

She shrugged and returned to the kitchen.

He sat up more slowly than before. The jacket he'd worn last night was on the chair next to the sofa. His shoes were lined up in front of the fireplace, which gave off much welcomed heat. He pushed away the thick comforter that had covered him. He was losing it if he couldn't even remember dossing down last night.

His head pounded. At least his vision was clear.

He found the bathroom, then went to the kitchen. The floor was cool beneath his sock feet, but the warmth of the house was so welcomed after their trek last night he ignored that slight cold.

Jake looked at the two people sitting at a small table in front of a window that overlooked a winter wonderland. The trees were snow-covered, sparkling in the sunlight. He almost needed dark glasses.

"Sit and eat," Stephen said, dishing up a plate and setting it on the table opposite Kassie. "We ate earlier."

"What time is it?" Jake asked, glancing at his watch. It was after ten. He sat down and began to eat the scrambled eggs, bacon and rye toast slathered with butter. It was the best meal he'd eaten in a while.

Kassie sipped her coffee watching him warily. She looked at Stephen, then back at Jake. "I told him you were trying to kidnap me," she said. "He's wise to you, so don't try anything."

Jake ate steadily for another minute, then he glanced at Stephen. "Not kidnapping," he said. "Escorting her home."

"My home is on Red Leaf Lane," she said.

"Atlanta, then."

"Why would she want to go to Atlanta?" Stephen asked.

"Her grandfather hired me to escort her home. After eight years of knowing nothing about her whereabouts, he just wants to make sure she's all right."

"If that's so, why not come out here, see her at her work, meet her friends?" Stephen asked reasonably.

Jake paused and looked at him, then Kassie. It would have been a lot less trouble for the old judge to do just that.

For the first time he felt a genuine flicker of doubt about the assignment.

"Did she tell you she has a history of mental instability?" Jake asked.

"That's a lie," she snapped, slamming her mug down on the table.

Jake shrugged and took another bite of the toast.

"So why not call the man and tell him Kassie's here and let him come to see her?" Stephen asked reasonably.

"He won't come. He has no power here in Colorado," Kassie said. "He can manipulate things in Georgia that he couldn't get away with here. Once behind the walls of his estate, I'd be a prisoner again. And next time not so lucky to escape."

Jake sighed. "He's not going to make you a prisoner."

Kassie tightened her lips and glared at him. Jake ignored her and finished his breakfast.

Stephen leaned back in his chair looking at them both, then leaned forward, resting his arms on the table. "So Kassie, it's Christmas break at school, make a flying trip home, visit the man, but stay in a hotel. Don't meet on his turf. Let him see you're okay and then come back."

He looked at Jake. "That would work, right?"

Jake nodded. Taking his cup, he took a sip of coffee then said, "That would work. And I guarantee you won't be made a prisoner. He just wants to see for himself you're doing okay."

"You do know I wouldn't trust you farther than I could throw you," she said.

"Then we do it the hard way," he said, narrowing his eyes. "But one way or another, you're going back."

"In handcuffs?" she taunted.

"Where did that come from?" Stephen asked.

"That's what he did before."

"Before?"

Kassie sighed, and looked at her friend. "My dad died when I was twelve. From that moment on, I was told what to do, where to go, what friends to have. My grandfather was manipulative, controlling and impossible to live with. So just short of my eighteenth birthday I ran away. Got all the way to Philadelphia, found a job and was set to make it on my own when he showed up." She glared at Jake for a moment.

His impassive expression did nothing to reassure her.

"He was a cop back then, moonlighting for the money. He flashed that badge, handcuffed me and dragged me out of the store where I worked like I was a common criminal. I sat the entire ride back to Atlanta in the back of his car in handcuffs. Once behind the doors of the old family home, I wasn't left alone for a single moment. Until they enrolled me in a girls school in Switzerland. I was three weeks away from turning eighteen. Three more weeks and I could have been free."

"Then what?" Stephen asked.

Jake drank his coffee. For all Kassie knew he was completely tuning out her recital of past events.

"At least I was away from my grandfather and his controlling ways. I finished college and then was sent back to Atlanta. Once again every move was planned for me. Friends, parties, receptions. Where I could shop, who I could call on the phone. If it weren't for Aunt Beatrice, I'd have gone bonkers."

"Aunt Beatrice?" Stephen asked.

"She's my father's sister. When he died and my grandfather got custody of me, she came to help out. The only friendly face in the house. Her and Jason."

"Jason?" Jake asked.

So he was paying attention.

"My cousin, Aunt Beatrice's son. He's a few year older than I am, was gone to college by the time my dad died, so his mom came to babysit me."

"By the time you returned home you were over twenty-one, why not just leave?" Stephen asked.

"I thought about it, but then things got in a muddle. I had no energy, no ambition. I couldn't hold a thought. I went through life doing what they told me, it seemed easier. Until I got the flu. I couldn't keep a thing down, and the muddled feeling left. I realized I was being drugged. So I pretended I couldn't keep anything down for longer than was true. I only drank tap water from the bathroom sink and granola bars I purloined from the kitchen help. I figured they hadn't been tampered with. As soon as I could, I left."

"And did a better job this time of vanishing," Jake said.

"Not good enough if you found me."

"How did you?" Stephen asked.

"Sara Montgomery. She thought she was helping you," Jake said.

"It was her credentials from the school I used to get this job," Kassie explained to Stephen. "She was a friend."

"Don't blame her, I told her I was working for an attorney and we were looking to find you were coming into some money but you had to sign for it. Told her everything would be kept in confidence. But you'd really be grateful for the inheritance," Jake explained.

Kassie knew her friend wouldn't have given her away unless she really thought she was helping. Next time, however, she would make sure she broke contact with everyone who ever knew her.

Sighing softly she gazed out the window. It was hard to start over. She'd done well in Winter Creek. She could do it again. But she didn't want to. She liked her friends here. Loved the teens in her class. She'd never get another teaching job without being able to provide credentials and she couldn't enlist her friend again.

"Couple of things you left out," Jake said.

She looked at him, "What?"

"I had reason to believe you were mentally unstable.

Who wants a sheltered teenager out on her own? I believe your grandfather was truly concerned."

"That's a lie. He might want to keep up appearances, but he doesn't really care about me. The problem with me was I didn't want to be there."

"So why is he so insistent to have you return?" Stephen asked. "That's the part I can't get around."

"Money." Jake said.

Both Kassie and Stephen looked at him in surprise.

"What money?" Stephen asked.

"I don't know, but if something doesn't seem right, money's usually the reason. Does your phone work?" Jake asked.

"Far as I know," Stephen said.

Jake rose and went to the wall where a phone hung. He quickly dialed.

"John, Jake. Did we do a background on Judge Sutherland and his family?...Run it for me, and call me back at this number. We've got a problem at this end."

He gave his partner a brief recap of the last twenty-four hours, then hung up and turned around. "We'll see what he turns up. In the meantime, Stephen if you can take us to the airport—"

"No way. I'm not going. What part of that do you not understand?" Kassie said, a mutinous look on her face.

Jake crossed the room leaning close so his nose almost touched Kassie's. "I always deliver. I guarantee you'll be safe. As Stephen said, you have two weeks off. We'll fly in, see your grandfather and you'll be back here before the new year. Guarantee it."

"Sure, unless those guys from last night find me first," she said.

"Ah, the men from last night. Another puzzle," Stephen said. He rose and fetched the coffee pot, refilling their cups.

Jake straightened. "No puzzle, they're after me."

"Unless they're from my grandfather, then they're after me," Kassie said.

"Who's after you?" Stephen asked Jake as he replaced the coffee pot.

"A man named Haley. I busted him my last year on the force. Broke up a lucrative prostitution and drug ring. He's been vowing vengeance ever since. With all the legal delays, he went to trial only a few weeks ago. I learned he got off a few days ago. And now he's making good his threat of revenge. Our office was destroyed, but we think he got to the notes on this case first and send some goons to track me down."

He glanced at Kassie. "Haley's not too concerned about any collateral damage."

"So one or both of you could be right. Either way, both your lives could be in danger," Stephen summed up.

"The sooner she's away from me, the better for her," Jake said.

Kassie crossed her arms over her chest. "I'm. Not. Going. Anywhere. With. You!"

Jake cleared his place, putting the dish and mug in the sink. "Thanks for breakfast, Stephen," he said.

Ignoring the two at the table, he went back into the warm living room and looked for his shoes. They were still a bit damp, but he put them on anyway. Glancing out the window, he could see their tracks to the house as clear as anything. He wondered if the men from last night would out be hunting them or holed up somewhere in town planning another attack. The sooner they left the better as far as he was concerned.

The big German Shepard lay in front of the fire, watching Jake.

"Your owner is one stubborn female," he said.

He rose and crossed over to the window studying the landscape. He hoped no one came down that driveway, but if someone did, he wanted the fastest escape route possible. All he saw was trees, snow and more of the same.

Could there be anything to what Kassie told Stephen? He'd known how close to her birthday she was when he found her before. He'd needed the money, though, and at that time hadn't cared how he got it as long as it was legal.

Being drugged could account for the way she looked at some of the events he remembered seeing her at. She'd seemed aloof, but drugged out of her mind could look the same.

Only it didn't make any sense. The Sutherlands were an old Atlanta family, old money. The judge was well known for his work on the bench and the philanthropies his family donated huge bucks to. There was no immediate money connection, but if John could turn up something, he wanted to know about it.

Until John called back, there was nothing to do but wait, and try to figure out how to get Kassie to go back to Atlanta with him.

He heard their voices in the kitchen, but couldn't make out the words. Trying to figure the best way out was not easy. Dare they try Denver airport? Would there be someone from Haley's organization there since the surprise attack last night hadn't worked?

He had a rental car to account for, too.

"We have a proposition," Stephen said from the kitchen doorway.

Jake turned. "About?"

"Come back and let's talk it over."

Jake looked at Kassie when he returned to the kitchen. She still looked mutinous. For once he'd like to see her smiling or laughing like she'd seen her at that lunch with her friends the other day.

He didn't remember seeing her that way since.

He pulled out the chair and sat. "Well?"

"I want to hire you," Stephen said.

"Can't. I'm already working a case," Jake said.

"When you arrive in Atlanta and Judge Sutherland sees his granddaughter, your assignment's completed, right?"

Jake nodded.

"Then at that moment, I want to hire you to guard Kassie with your life and return her to Winter Creek before school break ends."

Jake studied Kassie. Her eyes met his. He saw nothing to reassure him. "So we go back to Atlanta together?"

"With a couple of caveats," she said.

"Such as?"

"We drive not fly and Thunder goes with me. We tell no one we're on our way—no one! We stay at a hotel in Atlanta no matter how beguiling my grandfather sounds. And I don't eat or drink anything that's been anywhere near my grandfather."

"You're paranoid." Still, the first break in the refusal. It could work.

"Those are the terms," she said firmly.

"It'll take three days to drive to Atlanta. We can be there in a few hours if we fly."

"No."

He weighed his options. He knew better than most he'd have no luck dragging her on a plane if she was screaming and fighting him the entire way. At least she'd get back to Atlanta, see her grandfather wasn't the bad guy she's made him out to be.

Maybe she did have some mental problems. He didn't know. Judge Sutherland had a good reputation for his fight against crime. It didn't make sense he'd do anything to harm his granddaughter.

"When can we leave?" Jake asked. He'd get the job done, then take Stephan's money for the assignment and send her home after her grandfather was reassured. Then he and John would do what they could to go after Haley and break that threat. In the meantime, if they were driving, he could keep the shotgun with them. Just in case they were followed. That appealed.

"My car's at the house," Kassie said.

"Not safe there."

"How about I go check it out?" Stephen asked.

"They're the type to shoot first, sort things out

later," Jake said. "Still not safe."

"I've been around the block, I think I can get in and out without them spotting me if they're still there," Stephen said.

"And if they didn't shoot the car to ribbons," Jake said.

"Who's going to pay for the damage to my house?" Kassie asked.

"Try Haley."

"Ha, ha, very funny. You believe what you want, I know what I know."

Six

John called just before noon. Stephen had been gone an hour. Kassie stood by the window watching for her friend's return. Jake watched her, suspecting she was more worried about her friend than he was.

"Jake, I did a quick and dirty background check on the judge and family. As you know, the family has old money. Kassie's father had been Jonathan Sutherland, a wunderkind of some kind. He invented something that's used in most navigational devices, think GPS in every car on the road, and made a mint in his own right. The Sutherlands have been in Georgia since the Revolution and owned half the state at one time. Judge Sutherland's not hurting for money. And the fortune Jonathan made is tied up in a trust for his daughter. Couldn't get all the details yet, but it just grows year to year. No other heirs as far as I can tell. Want me to pursue that?"

"Might as well find out as much as you can. Anything else?"

"One son living, Samuel. He's a high end corporate attorney. His wife is Evelyn, very society. The Judge also has one daughter, Beatrice who lives with him. She's got a son Jason. Haven't found out much about him yet.

"Jonathan and his wife were killed in a bad single car accident. According to newspaper accounts at the time, it was just luck Kassie wasn't with them. One living relative on that end that I've found, Benjamin Cantrell, a cousin of her mother's."

"He live in Atlanta?"

"Yep, the whole family's there. Only Kassie's missing. You bringing her back?"

Jake started to answer in the affirmative, then remembered their agreement. He thought Kassie was being unreasonable, but he had agreed. "Some details to work out. I'll be in touch. Anything on Haley?"

"Cops are watching him. I told them he's our best guess for who would destroy the office."

"Brianna doing okay?"

"Yeah, she's working from her apartment. I got her set up with a new computer and cable service. We're looking for anything we can get on Haley or his known associates. My friend Bert at Central is keeping me informed on what Atlanta's finest are doing."

"Good. I'll check in again soon."

"I can reach you at this number?"

"No. I, eh, we'll be heading out in a little while. I'll call you."

"Watch your back, Haley's guys don't fool around."

"I know."

"Stephan's back," Kassie called.

Jake hung up and went to the living room just as Stephen entered, allowing a blast of cold air in.

"Jeez, it's cold out there," he said. He looked at

Kassie. "Sorry, girl, your car isn't going anywhere. All four tires were shot on the side and the glass is broken in every window. At least they didn't slash the seats."

"Small comfort. It'll have to be a rental car," Jake said.

"Nope, I stopped at the convenience market up on Ralls Way and stocked up. You two take my car. No one can associate it with you."

"You'll be without transportation," Kassie protested.

"In this weather, where do I want to go? If I need a ride into town, I'll call someone. Take the car, girl and get this settled once and for all. When it gets better, and you've been gone a few days, I'll get someone out to haul your car into town and repair it."

She gave the man a hug. "Thanks, Stephen. I don't know what I did without you. The insurance card is in the glove compartment. I'm going to miss you."

"You'll be back, missy. Come on, let's eat and get you two on the road."

By one o'clock, Jake and Kassie were ready to leave. Both wore caps, Kassie's hair tucked up under hers, and dark glasses, hoping to pass by anyone looking for them. Thunder lay in the back seat stretched out to enjoy the ride, her backpack on the floor behind the driver's seat.

Kassie drove. She knew the roads around town and had commented on Jake's lack of snow experience viz a viz his recent slide off the road.

He kept a sharp eye out as they drove through the outskirts of the small mountain town and on down the two lane highway toward Denver. He didn't spot anyone that looked like they were hunting them.

Once away from town, he began to relax. He wished he could talk her into traveling by plane. The trip by car would take a few days, even though the highway had been cleared of snow. The sooner he got her back, the sooner he could get on the hunt for Haley's men and the connection with the hit.

Kassie fiddled with the radio, stopping on a station playing Christmas carols.

"Tomorrow's Christmas," she said. She always loved hearing the carols.

"This trip isn't the way I bet you thought you'd spend the day," he said, leaning back against the seat. He could still feel the effects of the last couple of days, but looking at Kassie was pure pleasure.

"Nor you," she returned.

"No plans," he murmured. He'd probably have hung out with John. Or stayed home to watch any sports showing on the day.

She put the car on cruise control and stayed in the right lane, going just under the speed limit. The traffic was light. With the roads clear, it was easy to keep up speed. She hoped traffic would be light all the way to Georgia.

Jake studied her for a moment.

"What?" she asked, flicking him a glance.

"Just thinking."

"Stop looking at me while you're doing it," she snapped.

"I like looking at you."

She threw him a dirty look and concentrated on

driving.

He saw the color rise in her cheeks and stifled a smile as he turned to look out the windshield. If he had to bet, he'd say she didn't date much. Hiding like she was, she wouldn't want to get too close to a special someone.

The thought should have made him feel bad for her, but he liked the idea there was no one special in her life.

"How're we doing for gas?" he asked a short time later.

"The tank was almost full. We keep them full during winter because we never know how long it'll take to get to town if we have heavy snows," she said.

"Quite a change for you from Atlanta."

"We get snow in Atlanta from time to time," she said.

"I didn't mean the snow. I meant the entire set up. Not the fancy home you were used to, nor the conveniences of a big city."

"I loved Winter Creek," she murmured.

"Past tense," he caught.

"Ummm, depending on things, I doubt I'll return," she said with a note of sadness in her voice.

He didn't argue. Maybe he and John would look a bit more into the family dynamics of the Sutherlands. Could there be any truth to her allegations?

The miles rolled by.

Thunder stood up and barked.

Jake looked around, assessing each car he could see.

"He needs a pit stop," she replied. "There's a rest

station soon, boy. We'll stop soon."

"How do you know that wasn't a warning bark?"

"I know my dog," she replied.

Jake was glad to get out of the car twenty minutes later when she pulled into a roadside picnic area. Due to snow, and the light traffic, it was deserted. The dog ran to a tree and did his business. He ran around and into the copse of trees. Kassie stretched, leaned over and let her arms drop, then she straightened and lifted her arms over her head.

She was beautiful. He'd thought her pretty the first time he'd seen her, at that department store trying so hard to make a life for herself. Since then, she'd matured into a beautiful woman. Her figure was toned and shapely. Her hair soft looking, framing her face as it did.

He looked away, trying to see the dog he could hear running. He was not going down that road with Judge Sutherland's granddaughter. He'd tried marriage once, but it cost too high a toll.

But he stole another look. Her cheeks had some color in them and she lifted her face to the weak sunshine, her eyes closed.

He felt a stirring desire for a kiss, just to see if those lips were as sweet as they looked.

Thunder crashed back into the clearing, shaking snow off. He must have run beneath a bough and dislodged a cascade of snow. Panting slightly he ran to Kassie and sat in front of her.

"Have a nice run?" she asked ruffling his neck and rubbing his ears. "I have some water for you," she said, turning back to the SUV. A minute later the dog was slurping from a bowl she'd filled with water.

Jake noticed she never turned her back on him. Good, she needed to keep sharp if Haley's men ever caught their trail.

"Want me to drive?" he asked after the dog finished his water.

He watched her weigh the decision.

"Are you up to it? No double vision or anything?" she asked.

"I'm good. Even the headache has dulled down to a mild annoyance," he replied.

She nodded once.

Thunder hopped back into the car and Kassie climbed into the passenger seat, shutting her door with a bang.

At least he had something to do, even if it was only putting as many miles from her place as he could before they had to stop for the night.

As the hours dragged by, Jake kept the car at a steady pace, just over the speed limit, but not by enough to attract attention. The last thing either of them wanted was any kind of notice.

When it got dark he asked if she wanted to stop, but she said she wanted to push on.

Finally hunger caused him to slow down at an old truck stop on the highway just outside Salina, Kansas.

"I need to stop for food," he said, glancing at the gas gauge. "And we could use gas."

"Okay." She hadn't spoken in more than an hour. He wished he knew what she was thinking. He was alert for her trying to escape again, but she seemed resigned to returning to Atlanta. Was it only a trick to lull his suspicion?

He pulled in by the gas pumps.

"I need to use the Ladies," she said. "Thunder, wait. As soon as I get back, I'll take you for a walk."

She headed inside.

Pocketing the keys, Jake turned to fill the gas tank. Cleaning the windows, he looked at the various big rigs parked in diagonal formation. He checked the cars pulling in off the highway and didn't feel any of the drivers were interested in him or their vehicle. So far so good.

Once the tank was full, he pulled the car nearer the building. He could use a pit stop himself, but wouldn't leave the dog alone.

Kassie came out a minute later and smiled at the dog who was sitting up by the window, barking.

Snapping on a leash, she headed to a grassy area near the perimeter. Jake used the time to visit the facilities. Coming out, he spotted her still with the dog on the grass.

He called John from the payphone near the convenience store.

"Where are you, man, I was beginning to think you weren't going to going to call in again," his partner said when he answered the phone. "Do you know how late it is?"

"Yeah, but I can't help the time difference. I'll make this short. What's the latest on Haley?"

"The cops can't pin anything on him. According to

Bert they're as pissed as we are. Only I don't think they have anyone shooting at them. What's going on at your end?"

Jake was tempted to fill in his partner, but he knew better. Surveillance techniques were available to anyone with enough money. He wasn't going to risk Haley's goons learning they were homeward bound from this call.

"I know I hate snow."

John laughed. "Tell me something I don't know. What's the status with the granddaughter? You going to bring her in or what?"

"I'm working on it. How's Brianna?"

"Still mad as hell. She's more focused on finding Haley's connection to the destruction of the office than I am, I think. Anyway, she's got a new kick-ass computer and is hacking all kind of databases trying to find the link. Glad she's operating out of her place. If the cops catch her, I don't want it reflecting on the agency."

Jake shook his head. "You'd go through hell for her. Don't worry, she won't get caught. Look, I don't know when I can call again. But you'll hear from me sometime tomorrow."

Kassie had her head bent as she talked to her dog, but they were heading back to the car. Jake didn't want her to know he was taking with John.

"Gotcha. We'll get as much intel as we can get between now and then. Just toss the girl over your shoulder and bring her home."

"Oh, and TSA wouldn't find that interesting?" He could almost imagine the scene at an airport. It'd probably make the news and any hope of sneaking back to Atlanta without alerting Haley would vanish.

He hung up and headed for the car making it back just before Kassie. The wind was bitingly cold. He would be glad to get back in the car—or head for the restaurant. Some place warm.

"Want to get a bite to eat here?" he asked.

She nodded. "Let me feed Thunder first." She opened the back of the SUV and pulled out a container with kibble. Filling the bowl she'd used for water earlier, she placed it on the pavement for the big dog to eat.

Jake kept an eye out for anything suspicious, but no one paid them any attention. He wondered if they should push on through the night or stop some place. His body was crying for rest. He knew he was pushing things, but his sense of urgency continued to grow.

As soon as they finished eating, they got back on the road. He had the heater on full blast and soon was warm again.

"I hope we're stopping somewhere. I'm tired and can't keep awake all night," Kassie said a short time later.

He glanced at her. "Okay, look for a vacancy sign if we pass a motel."

The darkness cocooned them. Lights filled the car when another car came up behind them. Some dropped back, others passed. Jake was getting tired. He had a hard time focusing. Maybe he did have a slight concussion. He needed to get off or they'd likely end up in a ditch, or worse.

"Up ahead on the right, a motel with the vacancy sign flashing," she said.

He pulled into the motel and stopped by the office.

"No credit cards," he said as he turned off the engine.

"What?"

"They can be traced. I'm not taking a chance."

"You're as paranoid as I am," she said with a grin. "Got enough cash?"

He nodded. Taking the keys, he told her to wait in the car.

He might have known she wouldn't listen. When he returned, she was walking the dog on the grassy berm near the highway. Cars whizzed by. No one stopped or pulled in behind them. She was a perfect target, he thought, wondering what part of keeping a low profile she didn't get.

"One room left, two double beds, though," he said, walking over to her. "You about ready to turn in?"

She nodded, eying him suspiciously. "Only one room?"

He nodded.

"Then I'll sleep in the car."

He almost laughed. He was dead on his feet. If she was worried about her virtue, she could rest easy. All he wanted right now was a bed.

"And freeze to death over night? It would be a shame to let the room go to waste. You'll be safe and warm inside."

"I'm not so sure about the safe part."

"Worried about me?" he asked, his jaw clenching. Just for an instant he pictured the two of them tangled in sheets. But the way he felt, the only sheets he wanted tangled were beneath him while he crashed.

"Should I be?"

If he felt better, if they were traveling under different circumstances, damn straight she should. But tonight–

"I'm bushed. All I want to do is get a good eight hours of sleep in before we hit the road again tomorrow. You'll have your guard dog, what more do you need?"

"Nothing," she said. "Except my backpack. It has essentials in it."

Jake drove behind the first building finding an empty parking space near the perimeter in the darkest part of the lot. Which suited him fine.

The room was bare bones. Two beds, one bathroom, a flat screen television and a clock radio.

"You take the bathroom first," he said, after checking it out. The window was too narrow for her or the dog to get through. The door would be the only way out.

"I can wait, you look like you need to get to bed before you fall down," she said, staring at him.

He wasn't going to argue. He shrugged out of his jacket and headed in. When he came out, she was sitting on the bed farthest from the bathroom, petting her dog.

"Where are the car keys?" she asked.

"I have them." He patted his pocket. He didn't relish sleeping with them, but he wasn't leaving them out anywhere she could get in the night. He didn't trust her any farther than he could throw her.

Kassie stepped into the bathroom and locked the door behind her. She ran the water until it was warm and washed her face, studying herself in the mirror. She looked like death warmed over. Her eyes were red, her skin blotchy. She was so tired she could hardly stay upright. Not that she would give a hint of weakness to the man determined to return her to her family.

And with his pocketing the keys, it was unlikely she could get away tonight. That suited her fine. She just wanted to sleep until daybreak.

She still had time to find a way to escape. Once she had Stephan's keys. It had been a mistake letting Jake drive. She hoped she had a chance in the morning to take back the car. It was her only hope of escape. Unless they reached a city where she might find another way.

Thunder was a problem. She could not, would not leave him. A woman with a dog was a lot more memorable than a woman traveling alone.

Maybe something would come to her tonight.

When Kassie stepped out of the bathroom, she was startled to see Jake on a mattress blocking the door. He had moved the mattress from his bed, covers and all, to the floor. It barely fit between the end of the beds and the door.

"Making sure you don't take off during the night. I'm too tired to keep watch," he said. His eyes were already closed and she could tell he was about to drop off.

Okay, so maybe that had been one thought she'd come up with, sneaking out while he slept. She thought she might even remember how to hot wire a car. Her cousin Jason had taught her that the first summer she'd lived with her grandfather after her folks died.

On the other hand, she was so tired, she was glad she didn't have a chance to get away tonight. Tomorrow she'd come up with something. She pulled out her phone.

"What are you doing?" he asked.

Did he have radar, his eyes were still closed.

"I need to call my friend Eileen. We were planning to get together Christmas and I don't want her to come to my house and see the damage," she said.

"Don't tell her where we're going."

"Hey, those were my rules, not yours. I'm not telling a soul. Who knows who could spill the beans without even trying."

"Keep the call short."

"Worried I'll keep you up?"

"No, worried about tracking your cell."

Kassie frowned, looking at the cell. She had it turned off for the day, but it was on now. Quickly she pressed speed dial for Eileen's number.

"Hi, you've reached Eileen. You know what to do."

Kassie felt relief she got the answering machine. No need to get involved in a lengthy explanation. "Hey, Eileen. Kassie here. I've had a family emergency and am away from home for a few days. I'll call you when I get back. Have a great Christmas." She ended the call and turned off the phone.

"Short and succinct," she told Jake.

He didn't answer. She peered over at him. He was sound asleep.

She thought he might look less dangerous when relaxed in sleep, but that wasn't the case. His jaw was still tight. His eyes were closed, but she could imagine them opening in a split second if the need arose.

She switched off the light. Refusing to stare at the man any more. Refusing to give into the fantasies that briefly touched down. She wasn't sure if she'd go all the way to Atlanta with him. But if so, that would be the last she'd ever see of Jake Lancaster. She'd make sure of it.

With a vague regret for things that could never be, Kassie's thoughts moved on from Jake to her grandfather. She wasn't the naive young girl who first came to live with him. Nor the drugged young woman he'd bossed around when she returned from Switzerland.

She'd meet in a neutral place, let him see she was fine, then hold Jake to his word that a short meeting was all she was obligated to do. He'd fulfill his role as retriever, and she could return home.

Only she knew she could never go back to Winter Creek. Once her grandfather knew where she lived, he could find her at any time. She had to get off the grid again.

She reached out for the backpack, feeling it next to her as Thunder jumped up on the bed. All she had in the world was now within touching distance.

Feeling safe for a little while, she let herself fall asleep.

Seven

When Kassie woke the next morning she heard the shower running. Sitting up, she received a wet lick from Thunder who jumped off the bed and headed to the door. The mattress was back on the other bed. She donned her shoes and snapped his leash on him and shrugged into her jacket. Taking her backpack, she opened the door and stepped into the cold, crisp morning.

If the car had been hers, or she had a second set of keys then Jake's taking one set wouldn't have stopped her leaving. For a moment she toyed with the idea of hot wiring the car and taking off, but by the time Thunder finished his business, Jake was standing in the door of their room.

He closed the door behind him and walked toward her. "I saw a diner down the road a ways, we can walk over for breakfast," he said when he was close enough for her to hear him.

"What about Thunder?"

"We can leave him in the room. We won't be that long."

Once Thunder was finished, Kassie went to wash her face and brush her teeth. Her hair could stand a shampoo, but would have to do for now. She left her backpack on the bed when leaving the dog. He'd be enough of a deterrent if anyone tried anything and she didn't want Jake questioning her on why she had it with her all the time. She hoped she wasn't making a mistake. All the money she had in the world was in that backpack.

The diner was crowded with truckers. They got a table near the back.

"Merry Christmas, what can I get for you folks?" the waitress asked, bringing coffee to their table.

Kassie replied with a Merry Christmas and ordered. She looked at Jake. He was still hurting, she could tell. He sat stiffly, moving slower than normal. When the waitress had his order, and left, Kassie smiled at him.

"You must have done something bad not to have a stocking full of goodies this morning," she teased.

"What about you?" he asked. "What's your Christmas wish?"

"Today, to go home and forget about you and my grandfather and men shooting up my home."

He nodded in understanding. Christmas wishes didn't always come true.

"I saw a phone on the way in," Jake said. "I'll be right back, I want to call John."

Kassie watched as he went back outside. She sipped her coffee and tried to think of what she'd say to her grandfather if they actually met.

Would she blurt out the question of why he wanted her dead? Ask why he couldn't leave her alone? Or just be silent for the meeting, asking for the assurance once he saw she was fine he'd leave her alone.

John answered on the first ring. "Where are you now?" he asked when Jake identified himself.

"Somewhere in Kansas."

"Click your heels and get back here. This driving home is for the birds."

"I'm in a frigging phone booth and it's freezing cold out here and if all you have to say is get home fast, I'm done."

"Nope, got quite a bit–Brianna came through though she'd rather be working on the Haley situation. It seems Judge Sutherland is a bit over extended."

"Meaning?"

"He owes more money now than ever before. If something doesn't give, he's going to have to cut back a lot in his lifestyle, or risk bankruptcy."

"That doesn't sound very prudent. Isn't a judge subjected to a background check?"

"When getting appointed sure, but he's had that position for years. And I don't know if your girl is right about the attempts on her life, but he stood to inherit the trust fund her parents left her if she died before she turns twenty-five. Now it's all hers. Does she have a will?"

"Doubt it. How much are we talking about?"

"Several million. Seems like her folks set it up so that a bank administers it. Interesting, don't you think that no family member was administrator? And nothing's been touched since the day they died. The earnings have almost doubled the net worth over all the years. Whoever is managing that at the bank is doing a great job even after their fees."

Jake stared off into space, trying to wrap his mind around a judge of Sutherland's reputation offing someone for money. Well, not just for money, several million was nothing to sneeze at–especially if one was in dire financial straits.

"Why is he so far in debt and for how long?" Jake asked.

"A while as far as Brianna can tell. It seems not all of his offspring were as brilliant as his younger son. He helped out his son Samuel one time, when buying into the law office he's partners in. His daughter lives with him and her son has a gambling problem. I think some of the bailouts came from granddad. He also made some pretty stupid investments that didn't materialize, some in real estate that tanked when the recession hit. The biggest hit came with the ransom for the kidnapping that now seems not to have been."

"The daughter went to live with him when Kassie's folks died to watch over Kassie," Jake said, thinking about that.

"Never left just because the girl did. She's still living with her father, and enjoying the good life. You've probably seen her picture on the society section from time to time, Beatrice Pearson," John said.

"The society page is not something I follow."

"Me, either, but Brianna does. Anyway, food for thought as you continue your trek across America. Brianna also has a promising lead on some drug shipments she's hoping to tie to Haley."

"Try tax evasion. It worked on Capone."

"Your ETA?"

"Tomorrow night, early the next day. I'm not sure. Then I need to set up an appointment with the judge to see her."

"Not taking her home?"

"No. The only way I could get her cooperation was to agree to neutral territory for the meet." He thought about the other conditions and did not plan to have the meeting at a meal time.

"We'll keep digging. Watch yourself. By now Haley's goons probably know you're no longer in Colorado and may be waiting for you when you get back."

Jake nodded. And his home address wasn't a big secret. Someone with Haley's connections probably had that months ago.

"Tell Brianna we'll find a motel near her place. There's a dog in the mix."

"She'll love it. See you."

Jake hung up, glancing around the parking lot. He was impatient to find out more about Haley's newest drug deal. He must be feeling pretty cocky by now getting off the other charge. By the time they reached Atlanta he'd bet Brianna would have all the intel there was. She was a whiz on computers.

Until then, he was stuck babysitting a woman who definitely had escape written all over her. Only his keeping the car keys had her still around, he was sure of it.

When he reached their table, breakfast had arrived. Kassie had started without him. He took off his jacked, hung it on the back of his chair and sat to eat.

She didn't say a word, just ate her way steadily through the eggs, ham, hash browns and toast. From time to time she took a sip of coffee.

"We need to talk," he said at last.

"About?"

"Money."

"Didn't you bring enough for breakfast? I would have thought your fee would include expenses to be reimbursed by the judge when you deliver the goods."

"Not that money. Your inheritance."

She blinked. "What are you talking about?"

Jake was good at reading people. She truly didn't know.

"Your parents left a trust fund for you."

She frowned. "They did? Why didn't I know that?"

"Maybe at the time everyone thought a young girl didn't need to know. It came due to you at age twenty five."

"I'm almost thirty."

He could see her considering the ramifications of the news.

"So any time after I turned twenty-five I could have had the money?" she asked.

He nodded.

"How much are we talking about?"

"Several million dollars."

Her eyes widened slightly, then narrowed. "Are you kidding me?"

He shook his head, his gaze never leaving hers. She

was astonished.

Interesting.

Before eight they were on the road again, Kassie driving. Jake hoped they could make some real time and arrive in Atlanta in the morning. They'd go straight to Brianna's and arrange the meeting the judge wanted.

For the first time, he wondered more about Kassie's allegations. Maybe they weren't the ramblings of a slightly wacko woman.

"Tell me about why you think someone is trying to kill you," he said.

"Not someone, my grandfather."

"How do you know it's him?"

She shrugged. "I just do."

"Kassie, I want to hear it all."

She flicked him a glance. "And why should I tell you anything?"

"I need to know, if I'm to keep you safe."

She gave a short laugh. "That's funny. You didn't believe me before. Why would you now?"

"Motivation jumped several million points when I found out about the trust."

"I still can't believe it. Why didn't I know about it?"

"A question for your grandfather, not me."

She was silent for a few more miles, then began to speak.

"You know about dragging me back from Philadelphia. My one break for freedom and I was so close."

"You were still a minor."

"For only three more weeks. Couldn't you have waited three weeks? By then I would have made it. But no, you had to drag me back and before I turned eighteen I'd been escorted to that girl's school in Switzerland which had stricter restrictions than most prisons."

"If that's all—"

"It's enough. Anyway, I didn't get away. And when I got home, I told you, I was drugged."

"So the flu got the drugs out of you system. Could they be adverse reactions to the meds you were on?"

"I wasn't on any meds."

"I thought—" Jake tried to remember all he'd been told about that first assignment. But his mind had been elsewhere at the time. For a moment he remembered the desperation, the futile efforts to stop cancer's insidious spread.

"What?" she asked, flicking him a glance.

"Maybe it was an assumption. I thought you were on meds because of your condition."

"I didn't have a condition. It was a lie. He got that doctor to make up something so he'd have control over me. I'm surprised he didn't have me sign away the trust."

"You couldn't until you inherited it."

"Did he bilk the funds?"

Jake shook his head. "He's not the administrator, a bank in Atlanta is."

Kassie mulled that over for a few moments. "So now it's all mine and he suddenly wants to see me again.

What does that suggest to you?"

"A lot of things, actually."

She glanced at him again. "Really? Now you're thinking maybe I'm not totally crazy."

"Could be there's a motive in all of this and money is usually the primary one. Tell me more."

"When I got back from Switzerland, he said I should plan to make my home with him until I found someone to marry. How old-fashioned is that? Even my Aunt Beatrice thought that was dumb. She urged me to get my own place."

"But you didn't."

"I had no job. My grandfather wouldn't hear of me leaving. And by then I think the drugs had started, I had no energy or ambition. It was all I could do to stay awake during the day. I couldn't find a job and so was stuck at home. Then the accidents happened."

"Accidents?"

"That's what my grandfather called them. First I fell down the stairs. I was tripped, but no one believed me. He was the only one home that day. I broke my arm. The doctor said I was lucky I hadn't broken my skull. I think that was the intent."

"Tripped, how? Where was he?"

"He was in his study when I was coming down the stairs. There was a wire or something across one of the steps. Looking back I think being drugged probably save me as I was like a Raggedy Ann doll flopping down the stairs."

Jake considered the possibility of the older man rigging something to cause her to fall. "What about others in the house? They could have fallen if a wire had been there."

"Aunt Beatrice had gone out to some garden club event. Jason was rarely there. He had his own place by the time I got back from Switzerland. He's six years older than I am."

"Jason," Jake said. Another possibility?

"I told you, my cousin. Aunt Beatrice's son. They came to live with us when my folks died. The judge thought I needed a woman's influence.

"So just the two of you home that day, you and your grandfather?"

"Even the maid was away that day. Rosalie was usually there every day but Sunday, but that day she had a doctor's appointment. Truly, it was just the two of us, so no one else could have rigged up something."

"There were other events?"

"I was shot at once when I was out riding."

"Near the house?"

"No, some distance away, actually. I'd ridden the horse fast for a while, then I was walking back to the barn to cool him down when two shots rang out. One nicked the saddle, the other I swear I felt swish by my head. The official story was hunters missing their shot. But it was not hunting season. So poachers, all the more reason no trace could be found, so the authorities said."

"Sounds like a reasonable explanation," Jake said.

"Except, the judge was away from the house that morning. I snuck into his gun room after everyone went to bed that night and one of his rifles had been recently fired and not cleaned."

"Suggestive, not conclusive."

"I'm not surprised you're taking his side of things, he's paying you," Kassie said bitterly. He watched as her expression changed. "But, maybe I can pay you more."

"I'm not touching that. I finish one job before I start another."

"But once you've delivered me, that job is done and then you can watch me until I leave Atlanta."

"Yes. As I told Stephen I'd do."

She nodded, apparently satisfied.

Jake wondered if the attempts were merely accidents that had fired up her imagination. If she'd been shot, there would have been a police investigation. Not something easily covered up.

It didn't make sense, however. The judge would be well aware of that. It probably was a hunter poaching and a young woman's over reacting imagination.

"Frayed lamp. Gave me a shock, didn't kill me. Slippery bath tub. I wrecked my knee when I fell on that one. But the one that had me leaving was the car crash."

"What car crash?" Jake was beginning to believe her. No one had a run of bad luck like that. A frayed lamp? In the mansion she lived in, not likely to just happen.

"I was planning to visit a friend who lived about two hours from Atlanta, up in the mountains near the Blue Ridge. On one stretch of road it's really curvy and steep, with no shoulder to speak of. Fortunately there are turnouts every so often. The brakes failed on the car. I almost went over the side. I was already off the drugs and knew I had to leave or end up dead."

"The brakes could have failed. It does happen." he said.

"On a brand new car? That one had less than five thousand miles on it."

"Your grandfather's a car mechanic? Tampering with breaks is not something the average man can do," Jake said.

"He used to restore old cars. He and my dad. They loved to get under the hood and tinker with cars for hours on end. I remember when I was a kid they'd spend weekends getting dirty. He stopped when my dad was killed. But he has the knowledge to damage brake lines."

"Anyone check the car?" Jake asked.

"I don't know. I was gone the next day."

"And how did you manage if you had no money or job?" Jake had a hard time believing a man would try to kill his own granddaughter—at least the man he knew by reputation. Even the few times he'd met the judge in person, he had respected the man.

She looked at him for a moment then shook her head. "I'm not telling that part."

Saving it in case she needed to disappear again, he thought.

"It's a lot of circumstantial evidence and nothing provable," he said.

"Maybe, but I don't need proof, I know he did it. Now I know why. First I thought he resented the fact his son was gone. But now I think it's for the money. That's a lot of money."

"Did he need money?"

"I have no idea. I thought he was rich. But is anyone totally rich enough not to want more?"

"Most folks don't kill to get more."

"Humph."

"He's not going to try anything when we meet."

"That you know of."

"You'll be safe, I guarantee it."

"One face to face meeting and then we're even. And I'll keep Thunder with me."

"I thought a neutral place for the meet. Maybe an outdoors location for the dog."

"Whatever. Then you never come after me again," she said firmly.

Jake hesitated. He couldn't guarantee he wouldn't want to see her again.

"I'm waiting for that guarantee," she said, glancing at him with a frown.

"I will never accept an assignment from your grandfather again," he said.

"I don't know why you did in the first place."

"I needed the money the first time," he said, remembering. If there were any truth to her suspicions, he'd regret returning her to the judge. But the information he had been working with indicated a teenager with instability problems.

"Did you see a shrink when you were a teen?" he asked.

She shrugged. "For a little while after my folks died. My aunt thought it might help with dealing with the grief. The guy was a dork."

"Did you know he did an evaluation—writing up a

diminished capacity letter that got my attention?"

She frowned. "That was the other stuff you kept talking about. It was bogus. There was nothing wrong with me but missing my parents and not liking living in Atlanta with my grandfather."

Spotting a rest stop ahead, Kassie pulled into the right hand lane and soon exited the highway.

"Thunder needs a walk. So do I. I'm not used to sitting for so long."

He nodded, thinking about the situation from her revelations. Had the man pulled a fast one back then? Thinking no one would question him versus a grieving preteen? As no one had.

He climbed out of the car, keeping his door open.

She looked at him. "Not going to use the facilities?"

"Give me the keys and I will."

She gave a slow smile. "Not too trusting, are you?"

"Not with you, Sweetheart."

Kassie looked startled at the endearment. Turning she let Thunder from the car, snapped on his leash and took him to the pet area.

Fair enough, she didn't trust Jake either.

Kassie grew more apprehensive every time she thought about arriving in Atlanta. She couldn't determine if Jake believed a word she'd said. So she not only needed to be on her guard for anything her grandfather might try, she had to watch Jake like a hawk. No telling when he might turn and end up going back on his word and turning her over to the enemy.

She looked back at him leaning casually against the

car, his door still open. No chance to jump in and take off without him. But she could out wait him. She would use the facilities, be ready to ride again while he'd be needing to go. She laughed softly, serve him right.

Pulling out her cell, Kassie was pleased to see there was service. She called Stephen.

"How you doing?" he asked after she'd wished him a merry Christmas.

"We're not in Atlanta yet. I need you to be my backup."

"How's that?"

"I'll call in every day. If I miss a day, get a hold of any trustworthy person you know and get them looking for me. I am not going willingly into any situation, so don't let anyone tell you differently."

'What's up?"

"I just found out they had some shrink say I was crazy before. I don't want them trying that again. I also found out the reason for the attacks. I'm an heiress. Who knew? Actually, my grandfather knew. I didn't."

"Write a will, take that off the table," Stephen said promptly.

"So just stop somewhere, find a lawyer and write a will?"

"A holographic one will hold up in court. Get white paper, black ink, write it totally in your handwriting and sign and date it. Keep it somewhere safe."

"I'll mail it to you," she said, already delighted with the plan. She'd make sure her grandfather knew of the will before saying anything to him. So if he did kill her, at least it would be for naught.

"Sounds like a plan, but don't leave anything to me. That would look suspicious if I had the only will and was a recipient."

"Okay, I'll leave it all to Eileen. So any activity there that I should know about?"

"Man your place is a mess. Every window is shot out. Bullet holes on the walls. I called the sheriff and reported it as vandalism, told him I was keeping an eye on your place while you were gone over Christmas. No signs of the guys, though. And he doesn't have a clue how to find who shot up the place. I didn't offer any explanation, either."

"So everything will be ruined by the time I get back if we have another snow storm." She was angry. That was her home they'd destroyed.

"Naw, I'll call on a friend and we'll board up the house, call for someone to take your car into Ray's. He'll probably have it fixed by the time you get back. The house windows will take some time. But it'll be as secure as we can make it."

"Thanks, Stephen. At least those guys are gone. I feel better about your being there. I don't want them coming after you."

"Take care of yourself, kiddo. I'll wait for your call every day. Tell Jake that John fellow called again and wants to get in touch with him."

"Okay, thanks again, Stephen, for everything. See you soon!"

Kassie made use of the facilities, taking Thunder in with her. Then she headed for the car. She didn't see

Jake.

For a moment she toyed with the idea of jumping in the car and taking off without him. But she'd never be free of her grandfather if she did that. She was anxious to stop for the evening so she could get the will written and mailed off. Tomorrow, they'd reach Atlanta.

Kassie and Thunder ran around the pet area until she saw Jake heading for the car. They jogged over to catch up with him.

"Decided to trust me?" she asked with a grin.

"Yes. We have to start somewhere. Want me to drive?"

She studied him for a moment, then shrugged. "If you want to. I called Stephen and he reported those guys have gone. No sign of them. He even had the sheriff out to the house." She debated telling him the extent of the damage, but it really wasn't his business.

"Your friend John called, wants you to call him," she finished.

"Let me make that call and we'll head out. Can I use your phone?"

She handed it over, walking away to give him privacy, still annoyed men could come and shoot up her place and get away scot free.

"What did your partner have to say?" Kassie asked when they pulled out onto the highway.

"He updated me on the other case we're working on." Jake hadn't learned anything that could benefit them. Brianna was still working on digging into financial records to see how they could get another slant on the situation. He felt impatient that he was essentially wasting time driving back to Atlanta when they would have been there yesterday if they'd flown like he wanted.

"They have us booked into a motel in Alpharetta, complete with dog and fake names." John had suggested it might be safer for Brianna to keep Jake off the grid where Haley was concerned.

"And we don't show ID?"

"Brianna's taken care of that. We'll meet her at a restaurant. I'm figuring on being there around dinner time, so we'll eat, hole up, and wait for John to contact your grandfather and arrange a meeting."

"Seems a long trip for a quick meeting. He could have flown to Colorado if he really wanted to see me," she murmured.

Again Jake thought she made a good point. He'd asked John to have Brianna check as much as she could on the judge's finances. Was money the reason for everything? Or had a run of bad luck convinced Kassie of something that never existed?

He'd asked John to also look into the incidents Kassie had relayed.

It was dark by the time they arrived in Little Rock. They had to stop at two places before finding a motel that allowed dogs. Once Thunder was fed and watered, they left him in the room and went to dinner at a nearby diner.

"I need to stop at a convenience store," Kassie said as they finished eating. The conversation had been innocuous during the meal.

"For?"

"Paper. I need a tablet or something. And a stamp."

"What for?"

She debated telling him, but maybe it would help all the way around. "Stephen suggested I write a holographic will, to make sure if anything happens to me, whoever kills me doesn't gain."

"Killers can't gain from killing someone."

"If it's proved they did it. The judge has some powerful friends. I wouldn't put it past him. This way at least the money will go elsewhere."

Jake studied her for a moment. "Good idea. I'll witness it. Maybe we can get the clerk at the motel to witness it, too."

She blinked. "I thought you'd think it was a dumb idea."

"Nothing dumb about it. Once you get back home, you can see an attorney and draft another one. But holographic works in a pinch. In fact, it's rather clever. You need to make sure everyone knows about it up front so there are no threats, if that's what caused the attempts on your life."

She nodded. "Should I just hand out cards?"

He grinned.

Kassie caught her breath. It was the first sign of humor she'd seen and the expression transformed him. She looked away, not wanting anything to do with Jake beyond watching her back and then leaving her alone.

She had friends, she didn't need any more—especially ones working for her grandfather.

He wouldn't be working for the judge once she was in Atlanta.

She refused to think of any ramifications beyond seeing the judge and getting back to Colorado. They were like ships that passed in the night. But there was no future with Jake Lancaster.

She glanced at him. "Why did you need money before?"

"What?"

"When you found me in Philly. You said you did it for the money."

He nodded, reaching into his wallet to pay the dinner bill. "My wife was dying. We needed the money. I moonlighted as much as I could and still spend time with her."

"She died?" Kassie had never expected that.

Jake nodded. "About three months after I picked you up. She fought hard, but it was ovarian cancer and the prognosis was never good. You finished?"

She nodded. Reaching out to touch him lightly on his hand, she said, "I'm sorry. That must have been so hard."

"It was and is. We thought we'd grow old together." He rose and headed to the cashier.

Kassie watched him, hearing the echo of his words, *grow old together.* Would she ever find someone she could grow old with? Or would she be taking off again once they were in Atlanta, to devise a new identity and lose herself again somewhere in America? Always afraid to get too close to anyone for fear of her grandfather finding her.

Eight

A quick trip to a convenience store procured the paper Kassie wanted. As soon as they returned to their room, she sat at the small desk and wrote. Finishing it quickly, she turned to look at Jake. He'd turned on the TV searching for the news.

"I left room at the bottom of page two for you and the clerk to witness. Do you need to watch me write it or just sign it?"

"Don't know, but I saw you write it. We'll head for the front desk so the woman there can watch you sign it, then we'll witness it.

As soon as that was done, Kassie folded the pages and put in an envelope, addressing it to Stephen. The motel clerk sold her a stamp and showed Kassie where she could mail the envelope.

A final walk for Thunder and Kassie was ready to go to bed. She remained apprehensive about tomorrow and arriving in Atlanta after so long, but in hopes of getting this behind her once and for all, she was committed to following through. Her expression must have given away some of her feelings because Jake looked at her and asked what was wrong.

"Nothing, or maybe everything. You're sure you'll stick by me until Thunder and I leave Atlanta?"

"I said I would. It's not the nightmare you keep thinking."

"Explain away the incidents before I left."

"Coincidence?" He really didn't believe that. But he had an equally hard time believing a highly respected judge would try to kill his granddaughter.

"There's that possibility," she concurred. "Once or twice. But you'll never convince me it was all coincidental."

"If they happened like you said. Playing devil's advocate, what if you misread the situation each time?"

"Unlikely."

He remembered the psych file he'd seen the first time he'd gone looking for her. Could her imagination have played such tricks she firmly believed it?

She frowned at him. "Now what?"

He shrugged. "Nothing. You'll see when you meet him he's not the monster you think he is. And I can't get around lack of motive."

"He wants my money," she said.

"I don't know. Brianna's looking into that. But there are easier ways to get out of a financial bind than murder."

Kassie wasn't convinced. She knew what she knew. She didn't forget the judge was paying Jake to bring her back. She could still get away, but then remembered Stephan's advice. Get this behind her once and for all.

Once she had access to the funds she didn't even know she had before, she'd make sure no one found her again in this life.

She took her backpack into the bathroom with her when she got ready for bed. Counting the money still remaining, she wondered how easy it would be to actually access the money her parents left without leaving some kind of trail. Maybe she should hit the bank and take out as much cash as she could and let the rest just sit there.

Once she learned in the future that the judge died, she could always come back and claim it.

She sighed and leaned her head in her palms. Life had been so great when her parents had been alive. Never once had any of them any inkling they wouldn't continue that way. Life was unfair at times.

But she was stronger than anyone suspected. She'd make her own way and keep the memories of her childhood close. Ignoring all that had occurred after their deaths. She was well over twenty-one now and no one could hold her against her will. She shook her head. Well, maybe. So far Jake was doing a pretty good job.

Jake. She squeezed her eyes tightly shut, trying not to picture the man. She refused to let any attraction surface. He was not someone she wanted to deal with.

Liar.

Kassie raised her head, dropping her hands. Okay, so maybe she was intrigued a little by the man. He was still the enemy and she'd do well to never forget. Once this was over, she'd never see him again.

The thought was vaguely depressing, but she ignored that feeling. She'd be free.

When she left the bathroom, she was ready for bed.

Jake already had one of the mattresses in front of the door.

She grinned. "Ever think of the window in the bathroom? I could have been long gone."

"Not without your dog," he said lazily. Sitting at the desk, he looked up from watching the television. "Hang in there, kid, it'll be over soon."

"Hoping I come out of it alive."

"There's that. Maybe I'll get John to meet up with us and take you to see the Judge. I'm thinking the hit's on me alone, not him or others in the firm."

"It's me," she countered, sitting on the edge of the bed. "Maybe you should include your friend tomorrow for more fire power."

"Fire power? What are you expecting, gunfight at the OK Corral?"

She shrugged. "You never know. I think we should tell him first off about the will."

Jake nodded. "A bit blatant, but that works for me."

She studied him a moment. "What did you tell my grandfather?"

"John's been in touch with him. He knows we're coming into Atlanta tomorrow and will arrange a meeting."

"But not when or where yet?" she asked.

Jake shook his head. "We haven't even established the meeting place yet. I think last minute to minimize exposure to anyone who shouldn't know."

"I thought you said your office was ruined, no one's working there now. How would anyone know if you don't tell them?"

"Good point. Still, I think we play this one close to the vest."

"How long do I have to meet with him?" she asked, trying to envision the meeting. If left to her, they'd meet in an airport with lots of security around. She'd say hi, I'm fine, leave me alone and be done.

"I don't know. Let's say we go for coffee and as long as it takes to drink a cup of coffee."

"I'll ask for iced coffee, I can drink it faster," she replied.

Jake grinned at her.

Kassie looked away but not before her heart flip flopped. He was sexy as could be when he grinned.

Whoa, there was nothing adorable about the tough man who had plagued her more than once. He was rugged, masculine, and sexy without trying. That didn't help.

She focused on her dog, lying near her bed. His eyes watched her and when she smiled at him, his tail began to wag. Owning dogs was the best way to go through life.

"Will the coffee shop allow a dog? I'm not going without Thunder."

"We'll find one with an outdoor terrace that allows dogs."

She nodded. Taking off her boots, she lay down and pulled the covers over her. She could last another twenty-four hours. Then be on her way back to Colorado. Without Jake.

Turning her back on him Kassie let herself

remember every encounter with the man, from years ago, to the time at her cabin, to their road trip. He had a certain code and adhered to it. Honest to a fault, she wondered if he really could comprehend how some people were not honest.

He'd been a cop, of course he knew.

Unless they fooled him.

She knew her grandfather had a strong reputation. If only people knew the truth.

When Jake headed for the bathroom, Kassie waited only a moment, then rose quietly and pushed her feet into her boots. Using hand signals, she called Thunder, donned her jacket, grabbed her backpack and pushed the mattress away from the door. There was barely enough room to open the door a few inches to let them out.

Once outside, she hurried down to the grassy area to allow Thunder to do his business.

She stood beneath the lamp and waited. Not disappointed--in only three minutes the door to their room slammed open and Jake ran out, shotgun in hand.

She hadn't expected that. She thought it was still in Stephan's car. Silently she watched him. Thunder came to sit beside her as Jake spotted them.

"Dammit." He put the gun behind him in the room and headed down the stairs.

Kassie stood her ground as he stomped over to her.

"What the hell are you doing?"

"Letting Thunder go potty," she said, a smile playing around her mouth.

"You think you're funny?" he asked, stopping mere inches from her.

"A mattress on the floor is no challenge if I wanted to leave," she said, tilting her head back to glare at him. "I wanted to show you that."

He glared back at her until, to her utter astonishment, he leaned over and kissed her.

Thunder stood and growled.

"Call off your dog," Jake said against her lips.

"Thunder, sit." Kassie kept her eyes closed, feeling her lips move against Jake's'. His breath fanned her face, and he leaned in again to kiss her. The coolness of the evening evaporated as heat surged through her. When he put his arms around her, she stepped the scant distance between them to feel his hard body against hers. For endless moments the kiss consumed her. She felt alive as never before. Could the moment last forever?

Jake pulled back and looked down at her. "This complicates things."

"Great, just what a woman wants to hear that she's a complication." She struggled for a moment and broke free. "Come on Thunder, time for bed." She headed for the stairs as Jake fell into step beside her.

"I didn't say you are a complication," he grumbled as they climbed the stairs.

Kassie ignored him, trying to get her emotions under some kind of control before they entered the light in the bedroom. The sporadic illumination in the parking lot hid as much as it revealed. She did not want to have every aspect of her feelings on display once back in their room.

Her point had been made.

His had a greater impact.

Once inside, she tossed her backpack on the bed and shrugged out of her jacket, avoiding any glance at Jake.

He caught her arms when the jacket dropped to the floor and turned her around. She kept her eyes firmly on his throat until his finger raised her chin. Annoyed with herself, she looked him fully in the eyes.

"Kassie," he said softly, his gaze searching for what? Confirmation the kiss had been special? Had evoked longings she was desperately trying to quell?

"What?" she snapped. She did not want this conversation. Why couldn't he be relationship allergic and want to avoid any tete-a-tetes?

He remained silent, studying her, then sighed softly. "Nothing. Get some sleep."

Jake released her and turned to push the mattress against the door again.

"We'll leave early and be in Atlanta by lunch time. A call to the judge and you'll be on your own by dinner," Jake said, avoiding eye contact.

Kassie pulled off her boots a second time and got under the covers. The room went dark, but sleep was evasive. She relived their kiss, a longing for more almost overwhelming her good sense. She toyed with the idea of flinging off the covers, stripping naked and jumping his bones.

Another woman might be able to pull it off. But then, another woman wasn't a complication.

She wondered what his wife had been like. She must have been so young to die twelve years ago. She didn't think Jake was that old, just a few years older than she was, which means his wife had been way younger when she died.

And he hadn't married again. What did that tell her about the man, or the prospects of anything enduring coming out of this enforced time together?

Lots. None of it to her good.

Thunder plopped his head next to her on the bed and woofed softly. Kassie opened her eyes and stared at her dog. By the way he was moving, she knew his tail was wagging hard.

"Okay, okay, okay, give me a minute," she grumbled, closing her eyes again. She felt like she'd just fallen asleep. The dog nuzzled beneath the covers, giving her a wet lick.

"Yuck, get away, Thunder. You can go out in a minute."

"I'll take him," Jake said.

She flung the covers down and looked at him. He was dressed, the mattress back on the other bed.

"Hurry up and get ready to go. We'll swing by and get a fast meal and be on the road," Jake said as he called the dog and opened the door. Frigid air roiled in and Kassie pulled the covers up.

When she was alone she lay there for a moment, trying to wake up. She'd been tossing and turning all night, waking up thinking about their kiss, about meeting her grandfather, about what she was going to do next. About Jake.

Giving a growl of annoyance, she jumped out of bed and went to get ready. The sooner started, the sooner over.

As they approached the outskirts of Atlanta, Kassie grew more and more pensive. Jake glanced at her from time to time, but she seemed miles away, her gaze firmly fixed in the distance, her demeanor non conducive to discussion.

He'd called John before they left that morning. He was going to meet them at a restaurant neither had ever used before, but a chain that would suit for a quick lunch. That way, no matter who was watching who, they had a chance of anonymity.

"Anything new from Brianna?" he'd asked earlier.

"I'll get her to join us for lunch. How're you holding up? I'm glad this assignment is almost over. We need you back here. Haley's disappeared."

"What are you talking about, disappeared?"

"It's all over the news this morning. Apparently someone else got whacked last night and the cops were looking for him and he's gone. There's a BOLO for him. Think he knows you're back?"

"I don't know how he could. But I don't like the sound of it. Let's get this job settled then we can work together on Haley."

Jake pushed the accelerator even harder to gain a bit more speed. He knew Haley's haunts, knew his routine. He'd been after the man for years, and knew his former partner on the Atlanta PD would be working the angles as well. He'd call him once Kassie was safe. The only thing worse than Haley getting off, was his going off the radar.

He pulled into the restaurant parking lot just before

noon. Texting John they'd arrived, he sat to wait.

"Why are we here?" Kassie asked a minute later, as if just becoming aware of their location.

"My partner's meeting us here, he and Brianna. We'll discuss strategy and then call the judge."

"Thunder can't go inside."

"No. Take him for a walk until John gets here. It's cold today, and overcast. The car won't get hot if he stays here while we eat."

She debated, he could almost see the wheels turning in her mind.

"Okay."

He watched as they ambled around the parking lot in the rear. Thunder sniffed every square inch, stopping from time to time to leave his own mark. Kassie was constantly surveying the parking lot. He knew she was scared. He also knew he would never let her come to any harm.

When John's low sports car pulled into the lot, he parked several slots away. Jake got out of the jeep as John climbed out of his car.

"Kassie," he called.

She looked at the man walking toward Jake and nodded, urging Thunder to heel. When she reached Jake, he introduced her.

"John Ashbury, Kassie Montgomery. Kassie, my partner John. Brianna will be here soon."

Kassie nodded but remained silent. She petted Thunder and then urged him into the jeep. Lowering the windows, she took her backpack and went to stand beside the two men.

John was as tall as Jake, and as well built. Instead of the dark hair Jake had, his was sandy, cut short though his expression looked as fierce as the perpetual scowl on Jake's face. She knew he was as strong and dedicated as his partner and the knowledge brought relief.

"Here's Brianna," John said when another sedan pulled in. A woman with long dark hair pulled back into a ponytail jumped out and almost ran over to them.

"Jake, I was worried about you!" She flung her arms around him and hugged him tightly.

Kassie noticed he returned the hug. She looked away. It did not matter to her what his relationship was with anyone. Only a few more hours and she was leaving, taking Stephan's jeep back to Colorado, but by a route unknown to anyone else. She'd call Stephen when she was close and he could meet her. She was going to disappear again and this time would leave no trace.

"Brianna, this is Kassie. Kassie, Brianna Hawthorne. Our computer guru."

"Hey, Kassie. Glad you got him back here safe and sound. And that you got out when you did. Those men don't play around. Damage is extensive to your place and I'd write your jeep off as totaled and get a new one. I brought you some paperwork to look at." She flashed a quick smile then stepped back from Jake and pulled out a file from a satchel she had slung over one shoulder.

"Lots of good intel on the judge. He doesn't seem the type to kill anyone–not when he can send them to jail for years and years. But then, he couldn't send you to jail, could he? No crime committed that I could find. Unless it's identity theft, but I didn't see anyone harmed by your using a different last name and if your friend said you could use her school records, it's not really theft is it? I haven't heard of anyone going to jail for falsifying an employment app. Though I've heard it threatened a bunch of times."

"Let's get inside and get lunch started. We wanted to set up a time and place to see Judge Sutherland today," Jake said, touching Kassie gently on her shoulder and starting the group toward the entry.

The aromas of the Italian restaurant had Kassie's mouth watering for lunch when they entered. Requesting as private a table as they could get—just by the entry to the kitchen, usually the last one filled, they quickly ordered and then John and Brianna spent ten minutes filling Jake in on what they knew about Haley. Kassie listened with half an ear, eagerly digging into her shrimp fettuccine Alfredo when it arrived.

She checked her watch and wondered how long before Jake would contact the judge and they could complete their business.

"Okay, time to talk about the Sutherland situation," Jake said, noticing Kassie checking her watch for about the twentieth time.

"Plan A, meet at a coffee shop with outside tables. She wants her dog with her."

"Today? It's freezing cold out and looks like it could rain any minute," Brianna said, shaking her head. "What dog?"

"This is not freezing. Colorado's freezing," Jake said. "Granted, it would go better if it had been a warm sunny day, but we get what we get."

"He's an old man, he's not going to want to sit outside today," John added, glancing at Kassie. "Your dog'll be okay in the car. It's too cloudy for any heat buildup."

"You're missing the point," Jake said before Kassie could speak. "This is nonnegotiable."

Both John and Brianna stared at Jake then as if one, turned to look at Kassie. She met their gaze calmly. She was calling the shots at last and wasn't going to back down.

"Judge Sutherland is selling off property. According to his bank records I hacked, he's recently paid down some hefty bills. He's respected in the legal profession. And there's talk of him retiring in a few months though from what I could find, his health is fine," Brianna reported. "Don't know what the circumstances were eight years ago, however, or even five. He may have needed money badly back then. He still plays golf, has season tickets to both the symphony and ballet. He and his daughter attend almost every performance.

Kassie looked at her closely. "Aunt Beatrice's still living with him? She came to be there for me. I thought she'd return to her own home when I left."

"Nope, she sold that place when she moved in with you and the judge back in the day. Never moved back anywhere as far as I can tell."

"Does it matter?" Jake asked.

Kassie shook her head. "I just have to readjust my thinking. I thought she came for me, and would be just as glad to go on with her life when I left. Actually, I thought she would have remarried by now. She's not all that old."

"You need us?" John asked.

"Probably not, but extra eyes wouldn't hurt. You looked into the situations like I asked?" Jake asked Brianna.

She nodded, flicking Kassie an almost apologetic glance. "Nothing on the fall, except she was lucky she wasn't badly injured. Car was sold shortly after it ran off the road. Cops only took an accident report, no reason to suspect anything but a lousy driver. Can't answer to the drugs or poison, but she was seeing a shrink for a while, and he could have prescribed drugs."

"Can't hack into his system?" John asked.

"He died a few years back and as far as I can tell, all his files were disbursed to various other doctors as they took on his patients. I couldn't find anything on non-current patients. Probably his family destroyed the files," she replied wrinkling her nose at his lack of confidence in her abilities.

"Dr. Baldwin," Kassie said slowly. "He was the one they sent me to, supposedly to help me deal with my grief at losing my parents."

"And the one who wrote the assessment that you were mentally unstable twelve years ago when I came for you in Philly," Jake said, remembering the papers he'd been shown.

"That's wrong. I was never unstable, just grief-stricken. Why would he say otherwise? He never hinted to me he found anything other than ordinary grief. I only saw him a few times, when I was twelve. How did you have papers from when I was seventeen?" She frowned, remembering her sessions with the man and the different topics they discussed.

"Though Aunt Beatrice did suggest I see him again when I complained about the accidents. I wouldn't do it."

Jake looked at Kassie. "We're good to go?"

She drew a deep breath and nodded. "Make the call."

Two hours later Kassie and Jake sat at an outside table near a coffee shop she'd never heard of before. They awaited the arrival of Judge Martin Sutherland. Thunder lay beside Kassie, his head resting on his front paws. She had a hot latte in front of her, but had yet to take a sip. Her back was to the wall of the coffee shop. Jake sat next to her leaning casually back in his chair, black coffee in hand. His eyes were alert as he scanned the area from time to time.

John and Brianna sat at a nearby table, far enough away to give the judge a feeling of privacy when he arrived, yet close enough to see everything. They were ready to respond to any trigger.

Kassie stared at the street, wondering if she'd recognize the car her grandfather now drove. He'd had a black one before. Maybe he still did. She really didn't care. Rubbing her hands against her jeans again, she drew a shaky breath. She just wanted this over. Stephen hadn't been right, after all. It would have been much better to never have to see the man again.

A car turned into the parking lot adjacent to the coffee shop. A gray-haired man climbed out. He went around the car to open the passenger door. A tall woman with champagne colored hair stepped out. Kassie caught her breath. She knew them both.

"It's them," she said softly. Her tension spread to Thunder. He rose up to sit, looking at the parking lot as the couple began walking their way.

A low growl emanated from the big dog, his ears were up and forward, his eyes watched them, his lip lifted slightly to show his teeth.

"Easy, Thunder," Kassie said, reaching out to grab his collar and rub his ruff.

Jake put down his coffee, stood and also watched the man and woman coming toward them. John and Brianna pretended they were engrossed in their conversation, but Jake knew John was on the alert.

Judge Sutherland's gaze fixed on Kassie and never wavered.

The woman at his side must be his daughter Beatrice, Jake surmised. He glanced at Kassie who was staring back at them. Her face held no expression.

"Hello, Sarah," the judge said as they drew close enough to talk without yelling.

"I go by Kassie, now," she said.

"Oh, darling child, it's been so long!" Beatrice said, rushing forward. She would have leaned over to hug her niece except Thunder rose to his feet, his growl louder. Kassie tightened her grip on his collar.

"He doesn't like strangers," she said.

Beatrice halted abruptly. "I'm hardly a stranger,

Sweetie."

"To him you are." Kassie made no move to greet either of them.

The judge nodded toward Jake. "Thank you for bringing her home."

"Can I get you two coffee?" Jake asked.

Kassie looked at him in horror. He wasn't going to leave her alone with these two, was he?

"No, none for me," the judge said.

"I don't care for anything except to see Sarah–I mean Kassie. That will take some getting used to. You look a little thin. Where have you been all this time? We've been so worried about you." Beatrice sat in the chair her father pulled out for her. He sat in the fourth chair at their small table, next to Kassie. Thunder sat, stopped growling, but remained alert at Kassie's side.

"As I said on the phone, I'm not sure why we had to meet like this," the judge began.

"Because that's the way Kassie wanted it," Jake replied. "I have brought your granddaughter back to Atlanta. My assignment is complete, wouldn't you agree?"

"Of course. Send the bill to my home. You'll be paid."

"Thanks."

"Where are your bags and things?" Beatrice asked Kassie.

"In the motel where we're staying," she replied, not giving any hint of how she was feeling.

"Oh, no, Sweetie, that won't do. Come on home with us. Your room is waiting. We've had fresh sheets put on the bed and everything spruced up once we knew you were on your way. I've already instructed the cook to prepare your favorite meal for supper and Jason will be so delighted to see you again."

"I'm not going home with you," Kassie said evenly. She looked at her grandfather. "You see that I'm well. I'm happy living where I do and doing what I do."

"So there was no kidnapping," he said.

"No. I didn't know you thought that. I left a note saying I was leaving."

"We found no note," the judge said.

Kassie shrugged. She didn't know what happened to the note, nor who had profited from her leaving.

"Whoever told you I was kidnapped took a chance and sounds like they made some money in the deal."

"Maybe an inside job, someone who found the note and took it?" Jake suggested.

"All this time you've been safe?" the judge asked. "Where? Doing what?"

For a moment Kassie considered telling him. After all, she had no plans to return to Winter Creek beyond giving Stephen his car. But then she was not out to make anything easy for him.

"Not Atlanta."

"This is foolishness. This is your home. Surely you know that. What happened to make you run away? Those foolish thoughts you had about someone trying to kill you were all in your head. Accidents happen to all of us over our lives. I hoped you'd gotten beyond that notion. Your room is waiting. Your family has missed you terribly these years," Beatrice said, frowning.

Kassie shook her head. "You wanted to see me. Take a look. Now you have. I'm done here." She rose. Her dog rose with her, his attention still on the newcomers.

Jake rose with her. "Get your drink," he said, "and we'll head out."

"Wait a minute," the judge rose, his face going dark with anger. "You were hired to bring her home."

"Which I did, you concurred. Now I have a new assignment, protecting Kassie from any and all harm," Jake said evenly.

"That's preposterous. There's no harm in her own home."

"It's not my home, it's yours," she said.

"Sweetie, we have missed you so much. You can't expect us to be happy about seeing you for two minutes in this cold weather after missing you for so long. Please, can't we talk about it? Make plans to see each other, catch up on what's been going on over the years?" Beatrice made a plea, her eyes filling with tears. "I for one am not satisfied with such a short encounter. Please, sweetie, for me?"

Kassie owed Beatrice a lot. She'd given up her home to come and stay with Kassie when her parents died. She'd helped her to the best of her ability. It wasn't her fault things went the way they did. For a moment Kassie wanted that closeness she and her aunt enjoyed before.

But she wasn't ready to spend the time to foster that.

Jake stood at her side, silent. She glanced at him.

What would he suggest? Stay another day and have dinner or something?

As if she'd asked the question aloud, he glanced at her. "It's up to you, Kassie. You decide, we stay or we go."

"We go," she said, stepping closer. Ironically she realized the man she'd hated for bringing her back was the one she trusted the most.

"Sweetie, you can't just vanish again." Beatrice looked between Kassie and her father.

"We know where she lives, that she's well and happy," the judge said. "If you insist on leaving, at least give us an address so we can write. Your phone number so we can call."

"I have nothing more to say," Kassie said. "I left for good reasons, nothing's changed and I don't want to have to defend myself against you another time. If you have anything to say, do it now, because then I'm gone."

"Honey, we love you. You're my son's only child. How can you turn your back on the only family you have in the world?" The judge looked completely perplexed.

"Easy, that family tried to kill me! That severed any bonds."

"Nonsense, no one tried to kill you." It was obvious he was impatient with her allegations.

"Sweetie, nothing's going to happen to you," Beatrice said.

"Come back to the house. At least give us this afternoon," she urged. "Jason's at work, but he wants to see you, too. Your uncle would love to see you, too. Please?"

Kassie shook her head. "I don't plan to spend any more time with you than this meeting. And if you ever send anyone after me again, better make sure they shoot better than the last guys."

"What are you talking about?" the judge asked.

She didn't reply.

"We had some men shooting at us, and she thinks they came from you. I told her they were more likely from Haley," Jake said.

"Aaron Haley?" the judge asked.

Jake nodded.

"I heard that case was dismissed. But the D.A.'s building another as we speak."

"The situation with Haley is a bit more personal. He's a wild card and no one knows where he is right now," Jake said.

"That's Jake's notion, I don't go along with it. How could hit men find him at my place in Colorado? He thinks because they broke into their offices, but I think differently," Kassie said, glaring at her grandfather.

"You think I sent someone," the judge said flatly.

She nodded once.

"I couldn't convince you before. I see nothing has changed along those lines. I would never hurt you, child, you're my precious granddaughter. All I have left of my son Jonathan and his wife. I only want what's best in the world for you."

"Then we're on the same page. That's what I want, too. Only my idea of what's best for me seems different from your idea. Goodbye."

She turned and walked past John and Brianna who

rose and fell into step behind her.

"Jake, do something. It can't end like this," the judge said, the anguish evident in his eyes. "She had that same story back before she disappeared. There was no merit to it. I never tried to kill her, why would I? I thought she was being dramatic, but if she still believes that, maybe I need to look at it again."

"You know the doctor said it was all delusional," Beatrice said softly, her eyes following Kassie as she and her dog reached the car. "Jason will be so disappointed."

"She's a grown woman. She came back willingly, or I don't think I could have brought her. Kidnapping's a felony." Jake said. "She agreed to this meeting, but nothing more."

"I know, but I thought once she saw us, she'd relent," the judge said. "Can you please talk to her? I'll even hire you as her bodyguard if that makes her feel any safer. I wanted to spend more time with her than five minutes on a coffee shop terrace."

"She's family. We want her home," Beatrice snapped.

"Holding an adult against her will is kidnapping, no matter who does it or for what reason. If she doesn't want to visit, no one can make her," Jake said. He started to turn to follow the others when he paused a moment and looked at the older man. "For what it's worth, judge, when I found her she was happy. She has a job she loves, friends who care for her and a nice place to live. I hope she regains all that."

"We care for her."

"Then maybe you should have taken better care of her when you had the chance." Jake turned and in only moments joined the others in heading back to the motel where he and Kassie had checked in. This job was over. And there wasn't going to be any need to act as bodyguard. She was free to head for home in the morning.

Driving gave him time to think. He tuned out the conversation between John, Brianna and Kassie. Unless she asked him to stay with her until she left, today was goodbye.

He didn't like to admit it, but she'd gotten to him. He didn't want to say goodbye. But his life was in Atlanta and hers was in Colorado. Besides, an ex-cop in a security company couldn't offer the Sutherland heiress any kind of life.

He frowned. He wasn't thinking marriage. Hell, he'd only kissed her a couple of times. He'd been married. He loved his wife. He still loved her. He wasn't getting married again.

"Are we all in?" John asked.

"In what?" Jake asked, feeling everyone's gaze on him.

"For dinner at the ribs place. Kassie's never eaten there and you know it's the best place in the south."

"The entire world," Brianna piped up.

"Is that your assessment?" Kassie asked him.

"I've never had better. Okay by me." A little longer with her, then they'd part. Heck, he'd even miss her dog.

Nine

Jake watched Kassie as she seemed to blossom during dinner. John and Brianna kept the conversation going with stories of their start up, bloopers they'd made, showing a lighter side to early problems they all encountered. Kassie laughed at several stories and showed her patented disbelief until they swore to the truth.

He nodded from time to time. What had been a problem at the time, now seemed merely amusing. He was glad to see her laughing and enjoying herself. Time to face reality when she returned to Colorado and her shot-up house.

"You go home yet?" John asked at one point.

"Not yet. I want to do some recon before showing up."

"Wise man. Heard from a friend in the PD that Haley has been sighted a couple of times, but only at restaurants and none of his associates were persons of interest. We need to get more on him, have him rearrested and sent away!" His frustration was evident. "If we could prove he was behind the fire at the office, we could hit him up for reimbursement of costs."

"Good luck with that," Jake said.

"I might have a lead," Brianna said. "It's amazing what people will send through the Internet. And nothing's safe there." She shook her head and grinned at Kassie.

"You're hard to track because you don't use the Internet. Was that planned?" she asked.

She nodded. "I know about electronic footprints. To stay off the radar, I try not to leave any tracks."

Brianna looked at her and then motioned toward the restrooms. "Want to come with me?"

"Sure." Kassie smiled at Jake and John and rose to accompany Brianna. When they were in the restroom, Brianna surprised her by checking to see that all the stalls were empty.

"Listen, I know what you're planning–to disappear again. I can help if you like, but don't you ever tell Jake or John," she said after confirming they were alone in the restroom.

Kassie looked at her. It wasn't too hard to guess her plans given her history. But she was wary of any help–especially someone connected with Jake.

"Why would you help me?" she asked.

"I know what it's like to have someone after you. I know ways to get a background that will pass cursory scrutiny, and help get you a job and a place to live. After that, you'd be on your own. But no one would find you because you wouldn't be relying on friends who might give you away. You and I have just met, we'll part never to see each other again. No one would ever ask me, and if they did, I'd never say anything."

Kassie studied the young woman, wondering what the catch was. She didn't know her as well as she knew her school friend who had helped out before. But the office was enticing. Could she trust Brianna?

"What would I have to do?" she asked cautiously.

"Hang around here for another day or two. I'll need a picture, and we can collaborate on a back story— one that'll be easy for you to remember. It's sort of like witness protection, but without the government involved."

"Isn't this counter to your business? My grandfather was a client."

"Was is the key word. Jake fulfilled that obligation. Now, you can hire me to help you. Only we'll keep this off the books so no one can trace it."

"How much?"

"Yeah, it sounds like money, if I keep it off the books. Let's just say I'm paying a favor forward. Someday you help someone out. That'll work for me."

Kassie considered the offer. It would be a life line. Getting a job without proper identification or work history would be impossible. Unless she wanted something like dishwashing, and even then if the employer followed the rules, she'd need a social security card.

On the other hand, could she trust Brianna? Why would she risk so much for a woman she'd just met?

"Think it over. The offer stands whenever you want to take me up on it," Brianna said, turning to wash her hands. She smiled at Kassie in the mirror. "I'm really only planning to help, not pull the rug out from under you at some time in the future."

"I'll think about it and tell you in the morning," she said. She wanted to talk to Stephen, find out about the situation at home and make some decisions. Since Jake first showed up all she really focused on was the meeting with her grandfather. Now she had to make some decisions about the rest of her life. She didn't plan to return to Colorado longer than to pack up and move. She'd miss her friends, but could not trust that her life could continue as it had been before Jake showed up.

Kassie knew Jake believed the gunmen were from some man named Haley, but she wasn't convinced.

Brianna handed her a card. "My cell is on the back. Call me whenever."

"Thank you. I might take you up on your offer."

"If you want to." Brianna smiled at her and opened the door.

When they finished dinner, John and Brianna said goodbye and left together. Jake and Kassie headed for the jeep and drove back to the motel where Thunder had been left. She wondered if her grandfather knew where she was staying.

She asked Jake.

"I didn't tell him, if that's what you're asking. Kassie, I want you to know when I stayed behind this afternoon he said he thought you were being dramatic when claiming someone was trying to kill you. He thought the various incidents were coincidences. But with you still holding to that, and the fact of your being gone and hidden for so long, has started him wondering if there was some truth to the situation. I still don't believe he was trying to harm you."

"Okay, you've had your say. He could be trying to fool you, did you think of that?"

"Maybe. But maybe not. Before you return to Colorado, you might reach out once more to talk to him. Really listen to what he has to say."

She shrugged. "I don't need to talk to him or anyone else. My life is elsewhere."

"And the money?"

She considered that. A few million in the bank would go a long way in helping her hide—until she needed the money and bank records could be tracked. Could she get a stash in cash? Something to draw on in case of emergency but leave no trail?

She'd ask Brianna.

When she considered that, she realized she was going to trust her.

"I still haven't decided about the money," she said. She wished she could discuss things with Jake, but where did his loyalties lie? To a former client like the judge? Or would he help her?

"No rush, it's been there all this time, I doubt it's going anywhere." He drove competently through the late evening traffic. Before long they were at the motel. She took Thunder for a walk, Jake accompanying her.

"Do you think I'm in danger here?" she asked.

"I don't think you were ever in danger."

"Oh, those guys in Colorado were just shooting caps?"

"Well, except for that. But they were after me, not you."

"So you say."

He drew a deep breath and stopped her with a hand on her shoulder. "I don't believe your grandfather tried to harm you in any way. Those men were hit men, Haley's kind of guys. You're safe. I wouldn't put you at risk."

Kassie gazed into his eyes, seeing only sincerity there. Dare she trust him?

"Okay." She wasn't sure she'd believe that, but it was obvious Jake did.

"So, you heading back tomorrow?" he asked as they resumed their walk.

"I'm not sure. Maybe I should do something about that money. Are you taking off now?"

"No, I'm staying with you. Remember, Stephen hired me. I made sure the judge verified my assignment with him was finished. Now I'm guarding you until you leave. Cushy assignment."

Kassie smiled. If nothing else, Jake was an honorable man. Her smile faded as she realized soon she'd say goodbye and leave. While she hoped she never saw him again, it made her feel a little sad.

Nonsense. She had plans to make and they did not include a private security guy in Atlanta.

"Mattress on the floor again?" she asked in a teasing tone.

"No need tonight. You're free to go wherever you wish."

"I am, aren't I? Just as I was free to come here or not."

"Hmmm." He wasn't touching that one.

She grinned at him. "I still wonder if you would have insisted if Stephen hadn't talked me into it."

Jake's phone rang. He glanced at it, then at Kassie. "Hello."

She watched him as he caught her gaze and held it.

"She's right here." He handed her the phone. "Your grandfather."

Kassie stared at the phone, making no effort to touch it.

"He just wants to talk to you," Jake said softly.

Reluctantly, she took it.

"This is Kassie," she said.

"Kassie, before you leave, I wanted to ask if you'd reconsider meeting again. Hear me out. I've met a nice woman whom I've asked to marry me. I'd like her to meet you and for you to meet her. She's someone I met not too long ago. I think you'd like her. If you could delay your return home another day, I could arrange dinner tomorrow night. Her name is Betty Collins."

Kassie looked at Jake, feeling closed in. She didn't want anything to do with her family. Jake's presence helped ground her. He was committed to watching out for her safety. And she was suddenly curious about a woman her grandfather wanted to marry. He'd been a widower since she'd been a little girl. What did this woman offer that he was going to get married again?

Darn it, her curiosity was growing.

"I'll have to check with Jake," she said.

His eyebrows rose.

Putting the phone against her chest, she wrinkled her nose. "He wants us for dinner tomorrow night—to meet his fiancee!"

"Your call."

She thought about it a moment, then nodded and spoke into the phone again. "Okay. We can meet you for dinner. But that's all. And at some public place."

"Great. Thank you, Kassie. How about Dominico's at seven?"

"Fine." She recognized the restaurant as one her grandfather often used for family celebrations. Sighing softly, she hoped she wasn't making a mistake. It would be harder to kill anyone in a restaurant. No stairs to accidentally fall down. No out of control cars. No chance to drug the food.

"See you both then." He hung up and Kassie handed the phone to Jake.

"Dominico's at seven."

Jake took the phone and nodded. "I expect you'll want a new dress for the occasion."

She looked at her jeans and jacket and laughed. She had her stash of t shirts in her backpack, and that was all. Nothing there suitable for Dominico's.

"I expect," she mimicked. The money she had with her would buy more than the dress and shoes she'd need. Tomorrow she'd call Stephen, visit the bank, and see how far she could plan ahead with Brianna's help.

"You'll have to go home for something to wear yourself," she said as they reached their room.

Jake nodded.

Kassie was surprised how much fun she had shopping

for a dress. She rarely wore one in her current life. It was easier to deal with teens at their active level in pants. In winter, warmth was paramount.

She went to one of the boutiques she'd used in the past. She'd get a classic black dress. Who knew, she might have an occasion to wear it again someday in the future.

Conscious of Jake standing guard near the door and of Thunder waiting in the car, she picked the first one she saw. Taking it into the fitting room, she was pleased with it once she tried it on. Now for shoes and stockings and she'd be good to go.

Jake opened the door for her as they left the shop. "That was fast," he said.

She shrugged. "I knew what I wanted and they had it."

"Tricia used to spend an afternoon shopping and come home with only one thing," he said.

"Tricia was your wife?"

He nodded. "I hadn't thought about that in years."

"You miss her."

"Of course."

Kassie wondered if anyone would miss her after her death. Maybe her friends would a little. But years later?

"I want to take Thunder for a run in a park," she said as she placed her bags on the floor in the back of the jeep.

"There's a dog park near my condo. We'll stop there after I get my things," Jake said. "Want me to drive?"

"Sure, saves you telling me how to get there."

Kassie gazed out the window as Jake drove quickly to a newer part of Atlanta. When he turned into a complex of town homes, she wondered what his place would look like. They all looked similar on the outside. Did he go for early bachelor, or did Tricia's influence still rule his home?

He pulled to the curb in front of a row of town homes. The lawn in front was neatly mowed. There were shrubs in front of two houses, and a stone statue in front of another. She guessed the plain one belonged to Jake.

Thunder jumped out of the car and she snapped on his leash. He walked beside her, head up, tail wagging slowly. Jake led the way. "Damn, I don't have my keys. I lost them in the car crash."

Kassie stopped. She had his keys. Dare she tell him? She bit her lip.

"I'll have to call John. He has a set." Jake pulled out his phone.

She reached out and touched his arm and shook her head. "I have your keys in the backpack," she said, handing him Thunder's leash and heading back to the car.

She could feel Jake's hard gaze on her as she quickly rummaged in her backpack and pulled out the keys she'd taken. She touched the gun and wondered if she should return that to him. Might as well. She didn't need it and it was his.

She tucked it in her waist band and pulled her jacket over it as she turned and headed back to his place. Thunder was sniffing around while Jake continued to watch her.

"You had my keys?" he said in a low voice when she came up to him.

She dangled them from her fingertips."

He snatched them.

"I have your gun, too," she said, reaching for it and holding it out to him.

He swore and reached for the gun.

Thunder whined and pulled on the leash, moving back toward the car.

"In a minute, Thunder," Kassie said, taking the leash from Jake.

Jake glared at her a moment longer then went to unlock the door.

Thunder barked, pulling hard on the leash. Kassie took an involuntary step backwards to keep her balance.

"Thunder, no," she scolded.

He continued to bark and pull on the leash. She took another two steps toward the car. The dog barked and barked, pulling her away from Jake. Was it the gun? Had the dog seen the gun and was warning her. He was a trained police dog, but he'd never acted this way before.

"It's okay, Thunder," she said.

"Let's get him inside and maybe he'll stop barking," Jake said slipping the key in the lock.

"Wait." Kassie said.

Thunder barked and barked, pulling back on the leash, forcing her back.

"Something's wrong. He's never done this before."

Jake looked at the dog, then at the door. Slowly he

turned the key alert for any unusual sound.

He heard the click.

"Run!"

He turned and started for Kassie when the bomb inside the house exploded.

The concussion knocked them down. Debris rained over them. Kassie felt something hit her in the back. She covered her head with her arms while debris fell. Thunder yelped when he was hit. Slowly she risked raising her head, looking around. Where was Jake? He was closer to the blast.

Fire erupted and seemed to engulf the home in an instant. People came out of the other homes on the street to see what happened.

Kassie slowly sat up, her hand still holding Thunder's leash. The dog came to stand beside her, licking her, his tail wagging. Jake was closer to the house and still down.

"Jake?" Kassie scrambled to her feet and rushed over to him. "Jake!"

He moaned and rolled over, opening his eyes. "Damn, this was my home," he said as he sat up and stared at the destruction.

"Call 911," he said.

"Already done," a man said coming over. "You okay?"

Jake nodded, reaching to the back of his head. His hand was covered in blood in short order.

"Let's get away from the fire, the heat's intolerable," the man said, reaching down a hand to help Jake up.

They moved to the sidewalk, more and more people

joining them watching the house burn. His next door neighbor wasn't home. He hoped the fire could be contained before it spread to her place.

Sirens could be heard in the distance, growing louder as the emergency vehicles drew closer.

Another neighbor gave him a dishtowel and he pressed it against the wound in his head.

"Gas leak?" asked another.

"Don't know," replied another.

Jake didn't say anything but glanced at Kassie and her dog.

"Thunder probably saved our lives," he said softly.

She nodded, reaching out to link her hand with his free one.

"Maybe those gun men in Colorado were hunting you after all," she said watching the fire.

Paramedics on site strongly advised taking Jake to the hospital, but he declined. They managed to stop the bleeding and placed a temporary bandage on the injury, checked him over for other injuries and again urged him to seek medical attention. They were worried about concussion from the blow to his head.

Kassie was bruised in a couple of places where falling debris had hit her, but otherwise was unharmed.

The police arrived and took their statements with a request to stop by the police station later to answer any other questions that might arise. Jake suggested the cause was the same as the bomb at their offices and the officer promised to connect with the detective investigating that.

The fire was contained and extinguished, without

spreading to adjacent structures. Jake and Kassie sat in the jeep as the responders worked. Once the fire chief came over to say they were leaving, Jake asked when he could go inside.

"I'll send a man in with you. Lots of smoke and water damage beyond the initial explosion. We're investigating the cause."

"Talk with the cops. It was a bomb."

"You were lucky, then."

Jake nodded, his eyes narrowed at the destruction of his place. "Yeah, I guess."

Kassie waited with the dog while Jake and one of the firefighters went inside. He came out a few minutes later empty handed. He spoke with the man and then shook hands. When he got into the jeep, she looked at him.

"Nothing?"

"Everything is either soaking wet, or not there. I think the force was directed more inside than out. We were lucky. And your dog was the factor. I'd have just opened it and stepped inside, never suspecting they'd bomb my place like the office."

"So we head out for more shopping?" she asked as she started the car. "Unless you'd rather see a doctor first?"

"No. We'll stop at a clinic later to get my head checked, but not yet." He called John and filled him in on the situation as Kassie drove to a mall she knew about. There was bound to be a men's shop there. Not something she was very familiar with.

In light of this bombing, she changed her mind

about thinking her grandfather sent those men to kill her. It seemed like Jake had been right. They were after him.

Not that she believed she hadn't been a target eight years ago. But apparently the accidents she'd had were limited to the Atlanta area. So did that mean it was safe to go home, to resume her life? School break was still on. No one in Colorado would have to know anything–except Stephen.

She still wanted to talk to her friend–bounce some things off him. He hadn't answered when she'd called earlier. Maybe he'd be by the phone now. Once back at their room, she'd give him a call.

Leaving the destroyed town house, they headed for John's place to meet with John and Brianna to discuss the situation. Kassie didn't pay much attention to the initial discussion, trying to figure out a way to get alone with Brianna.

Finally, Brianna looked over at Kassie as if she could read her mind.

"I'm going out for sandwiches. Want to come?" she asked.

"Sure."

Once in her car, Brianna turned to Kassie.

"So?"

"I may not need help. I thought the gun men in Colorado were after me. Now I believe Jake's theory, they were hit men after him. So maybe my grandfather didn't send anyone except Jake. Still, I dare not let down my guard. Once I leave here, I'd like to know I don't have to look over my shoulder all the time."

"Are you set for money?"

"I need to figure that out, too. Tell me about my trust."

Brianna gave her a great deal of information about the trust. Kassie didn't ask how she'd found out all she had. She was grateful she could make decisions separate from her grandfather knowing what she was doing.

"We can head for the bank now, if you like. But you need ID," Brianna said starting the car and easing into traffic.

"All my ID is in Kassie Montgomery. I don't have any Sutherland ID anymore."

"Then we'd need your grandfather or aunt to vouch for you. Unless the banker knows you personally."

"Is it Joseph Tomlinson? He was a friend of my father's I remember. He knows me."

"Name isn't familiar. Does he work at the main office of the bank?" Brianna asked.

"I think so. But it's been years, he could have changed jobs a half a dozen times by now."

"Let's give it a whirl."

They arrived at the First National Bank where the trust was administered. Kassie recognized the bank from when she lived in Atlanta. She remembered coming in a couple of times with her grandfather to sign some papers. She told Brianna that as they entered.

"You probably had to sign stuff even back before you could take it on. Let's head right for the trust department.

To Kassie's amazement, Joseph Tomlinson still

worked at the bank, now in a position of senior vice president. He responded immediately when told Sarah Sutherland wanted to see him.

"Oh, my, Sarah. You are a sight for sore eyes!" he exclaimed when he entered the lobby and honed right in on her. His smile was broad, his delight genuine. "The judge didn't tell me you'd be coming in. How are you? Where have you been all these years?" He gave her a big hug and then held her shoulders as he stepped back and gazed at her. "You look so much like your mother. I wish your parents were still here to see you. Come on up to my office."

Kassie quickly introduced Brianna and the two of them went with the banker to his office.

"I came about the trust," she said once they were seated across from his desk. "How do I access the funds?"

"You became eligible for it five years ago. You can fill out the appropriate paperwork and be ready to go. Plan on making any changes?"

Kassie glanced at Brianna who just shrugged. "I don't know. I assume it's invested in stocks and such. Guess I'll leave it as it is for the time being."

"You can set it up so you get interest only from the investments. We've been reinvesting everything, pending different instructions. Now you can set it up however you wish. Let me explain some of the options," he said, launching into several different ways to handle the investments and income.

"Can I leave the bulk invested as is and have the income automatically transferred to another bank? I live in Colorado now."

"Sure, however you wish to handle things. Marcella Pembroke is the gal handling your particular trust. You can meet with her and set it up however you wish. You have your account number at your Colorado bank?"

She nodded.

"Then I see no problem. Before I introduce you to Marcella, however, do tell me what you've been up to."

Kassie chatted for a few minutes with the man who had known her parents. She wondered what her life would have been like had the car crash never happened. Everything would have been so different.

But it had. And life moved on.

Once finished in the bank, it was late afternoon.

"Jake will think we left town," Kassie said as the two women walked to Brianna's car.

"If they even noticed we weren't back. Once they get involved in strategic planning, the rest of the world seems to disappear."

"So the money aspect is taken care of as long as no one traces the account," Kassie said.

"It would take a court order—which your grandfather might be able to do being a judge. But there are checks and balances and I doubt he could pull it off without someone noticing. So even if you move on, you'll have that income stream to draw upon. What kind of job do you want?"

"I love working with kids. I'm a teacher in a private school, didn't require quite the background check the state would have. They were desperate for a teacher when I was hired."

"Easy peasy. Give me a day or two. Any special name you'd like?"

Kassie gazed out the windshield. "No. Maybe stick with Kassie so I can answer to it. But I don't dare keep this last name."

"Then let's use Johnson. It's the most common name in the US which makes it harder to backtrack. I'll give you everything tomorrow. I'll need a bit of time to get the stuff together."

"Thanks, Brianna."

"I love doing this kind of thing. I don't get to very often."

Kassie wondered whom else benefited from all new identities. Considering it safer not to even ask, she merely nodded.

Kassie was famished when Brianna pulled into the parking lot by a sandwich shop. They bought their sandwiches and ate them on site. Then they bought ones for Jake and John before returning to John's place.

The men were still at work, but strategic planning had moved on to investigating and both were on the phone asking questions.

Brianna dropped the bag on the table and waited until John hung up.

"What did I miss?" she asked,

"We've got a lead on Haley."

"Cool. Where?"

"He's still in Atlanta, we think. Jake is coordinating with APD right now."

"Can they pick him up?"

"Not unless we find something new to pin on him.

We need you to track his phone records. We think he has a burner phone, but by triangulating his known whereabouts, maybe you can figure it out."

"Sure. Here's lunch." Brianna crossed over to her laptop and began typing.

John glanced at his watch and then at Kassie. "It took y'all this long to get lunch?"

"We ate there," she said and went to sit down beside Thunder. "How's Jake doing?"

"Headache he admits to, but nothing's slowing him down," John replied, then took a big bite of his sandwich.

Kassie listened with half a mind to the conversation, more concerned with dinner tonight. Her curiosity warred with anticipation. In retrospect, she should not care who her grandfather was seeing. She should get away as quickly as possible. But a hint of the child who had loved visiting her grandfather when her parents were alive lingered. For a few minutes she thought wistfully of what life would have been like had her parents not died so young.

But the past couldn't be changed. She had her own way to make in the world. She would share a dinner with him and his future wife and then return home. Realizing the attempts on her life in Winter Creek were really connected to Jake had her rethinking her grandfather. Even if he'd tried to harm her in the past, she doubted he'd try now that she had inherited.

She still had not told anyone about her will. She would do so at dinner–eliminating any financial gain to any of her family by her death. She considered that her insurance.

She watched Jake as he talked and jotted notes. He'd no sooner finish one phone call than he made another. John had resumed his calling and Brianna was focused on the computer. From time to time, she yell "Yes!" and toss John a note she'd dashed off.

Kassie was bored.

"I'm taking Thunder for a walk," she said. The dog rose when she did, recognizing the word, his tail wagging.

"Want me to go with you?" Jake asked, looking at her.

"I'm good." Time she was on her own again. He wouldn't be her bodyguard beyond dinner tonight. She doubted anything would happen to her in broad daylight, on foot, in this section of Atlanta.

She and Thunder walked away from the high-rise apartment building. She spotted a park a block away and took her dog there. There was no dog run, so she walked along the path, allowing him to do his business against the trees near the path. She had a few baggies in her pocket, but didn't need any.

"We'll be going home tomorrow," she told her dog. "You'll like being back in the snow." It was almost as cold in Atlanta as home, but no snow. She didn't get why Jake thought Colorado was any colder than it had been here these last two days.

Kassie felt more confident than ever in the cold sunshine of the park. She found a bench and called Stephen. He answered on the first ring.

She brought him up date on what had been

happening.

"And you're okay with seeing your family again tonight?" he asked after she finished.

"I think so. I mean, everyone there knows I've accused the judge. I can't imagine anything happening that wouldn't go right back to him. I wrote a holographic will and mailed it to you, did you get it yet? I plan to get a formal one done as soon as I get home. Jake said that should eliminate any motive for my death. I don't know, Stephen, it feels weird to be here. I'm more than ready to get home."

"You'll have a mess to clean up. I called the glass people and the windows will be replaced next week. They had to special order some because your sizes are uncommon. Want me to get one of those disaster cleaners in to get the place more habitable?"

"If you would that'd be great. I especially need all the glass removed so Thunder doesn't cut his paws. I'll stay with someone if I get back before they can clean the place. It'll take me three or four days to drive back. I won't have anyone to switch off driving with."

"Take your time. But keep safe."

"I'm doing my best."

Jake was pacing the living room when she entered the apartment a few minutes later. "What took you so long?" he asked, coming over to her.

Kassie was surprised. "I called Stephen while I sat in the park for a while. Some of the kids there made a fuss over Thunder. He loves that kind of attention. Did

I miss something?"

"No." He studied her face then turned away. "I was worried about you."

"Thanks, but I was fine. I doubt the judge would try anything in broad daylight."

He shook his head. "I still find it hard to believe Judge Sutherland would ever try to kill a member of his family."

"So are you going to the dark side, discounting what I know?" she asked, her heart dropping.

"Nope, just wondering if there is another aspect we're missing."

"You two are meeting the judge tonight, right?" John asked, looking up from his laptop. "Maybe you can ask some questions at some point in time and see what turns up. I'd investigate the shrink angle. Why did that guy say you were crazy if you weren't?"

Kassie brightened. "Maybe I could ask him that myself.

"Nope," Brianna called, her eyes still on her monitor. "He died several months after you disappeared. We tried that angle already."

"Can we get a court order for the records?" Kassie asked.

"If you find a judge who would do it. And if we can find out if those records still exist. They may have been destroyed."

"Or scattered among those taking on his clients," Jake said.

"Except, she was no longer a client at the time of his death. Still, the files may have been transferred to one of the other doctors." John said.

"Something worth looking into," Jake said.

"I'm on it," Brianna said. "Find out all you can tonight about the doctor, who recommended him, why did you go there in the first place? Who had access to him? Once you turned eighteen, no one else should have had any access."

"I didn't see him after my thirteenth birthday. That's what's so weird about a letter from him when I was seventeen."

She flicked a glance to Jake. "Even if they thought I needed a shrink after my trip to Baltimore, I was shipped off to Switzerland and that girls school days before I would have turned eighteen."

He nodded, his expression serious. "Another suspicious act, but not life-threatening."

She shrugged. "No incidents in Switzerland. What does that tell you?"

"We better get going if we're going to get cleaned up before dinner. I need a shower," Jake said.

She nodded.

"We'll reconvene in the morning," John said. "Y'all have fun."

Ten

When Kassie entered their room from the bathroom Jake turned from the dresser and looked at her. She was the beautiful socialite he remembered from before. The black dress she wore skimmed across her figure like a loving skin, following the contours faithfully, stopping just short of her knees. Her legs were amazing. He only had seen her in jeans this trip. He caught his breath at how lovely she was.

She should not feel the need to hide away in some small western town. If nothing else, he wanted her to feel safe enough to live anywhere and pursue whatever she wanted in life.

"You look beautiful," he said.

She looked at him in genuine surprise. "Thank you. You clean up pretty good yourself," she replied.

The dark gray suit he'd bought didn't fit as well as his others had. But time was the critical issue and he didn't have any to wait for a tailor. Once his insurance claim was settled, he'd have to get an entire new wardrobe. But for tonight, this suit would do.

"Ready?"

"As I'll ever be, I guess," she said. She petted

Thunder. "He'll be okay here, right?"

"Don't see why not. Beats waiting in the car all night."

She donned her ski jacket, grinning at him.

"Not quite the compliment to the dress," she said.

He shook his head. "We should have thought about a coat, too."

"Naw, I might wear this dress again, I doubt I'd ever wear a coat to go with it. I live simple in Colorado."

Stepping into Dominica's a short time later Kassie felt as if she were stepping into her past. Her family had often dined at the famous restaurant. Nothing appeared to have changed. The voices were quiet, the atmosphere rarefied. Starched white linen table cloths covered tables, the silverware gleamed in the light. Crystal glassed awaited fine wines. Even the carpet underfoot was luxurious.

"Joining the Sutherland party," Jake told the maitre d', slipping Kassie's jacket from her shoulders and handing it to the coat check girl.

"Of course, this way please."

When they approached the table Kassie noted it was at the edge of the room, discretely away from the majority of those dining. Her grandfather was talking with a woman several years younger, with salt-and-pepper hair. Aunt Beatrice was talking with her son Jason. She spotted Kassie first and said something to Jason. He turned quickly, a smile crossing his face. Rising, he stepped out to greet her.

"Sarah! You're prettier than you've ever been." He

gave her a big hug. "Glad you decided to stay over so we could see each other. It's been too long!"

"Hi Jason." She stepped back, feeling overwhelmed. "This is Jake Lancaster. And I go by Kassie now, not Sarah."

"Ah, the bodyguard. You won't have much work around this group," Jason said offering his hand. His eyes assessed and in a moment he turned back to the table. "I take it you two haven't met Betty yet, since Mom and I only met her a few minutes ago. The judge still likes to throw out surprises."

Kassie and Jake were introduced by the judge who rose when Kassie came up to the table.

Betty Collins seemed flustered by the attention. Her smile was sweet and it was obvious she was in love with Judge Sutherland.

"It's so nice to meet you, Kassie. I know Martin is so pleased to learn you're doing so well. Thank you for staying over so we could meet. Maybe you could return for a quick trip for the wedding. It will be in April. Spring in Atlanta is so beautiful."

"Nice to meet you," Kassie responded, not answering the invitation. She sat when Jake held her chair, next to Jason. He went around the table and sat next to her aunt, who sat at the foot of the table opposite her father.

"Such short notice," Beatrice said with a smile. "I do hope you can get everything done in time."

"We are not having a large ceremony, just a few close friends," Betty said. "And family, of course."

Beatrice smiled, but Kassie could tell it was an

effort. Interesting that she had not met Betty prior to this evening. How did she feel knowing her father was remarrying after all these years? She'd no longer be the hostess of their home.

Betty kept the conversation going during the dinner. When asked, she told about her work as an ER nurse at one of Atlanta's busiest hospitals.

Jason brought Kassie up to date on his life, complaining about the job he had with an insurance firm.

"They won't let me move up as fast as I want. I might leave and find another place to work."

"That's your fourth job," the judge said. "Nothing moves employees up as fast as you seem to expect."

Jason nodded, obviously irked by the judge's comment. He flicked a conspiratorial glance at Kassie and said under his breath, "He thinks everyone should be an apprentice until their fifties when they may be old enough to assume more responsibility."

When Betty turned her attention to Jake and asked what exactly his job was, everyone at the table seemed to go on alert.

"Primarily provide security for local businesses and businessmen."

"Including finding lost granddaughters," Jason said.

"That was a special deal—a favor to the judge," he said, his gaze on Kassie. "Tonight I'm back to providing security for Kassie."

"And is acting as a bodyguard really necessary?" Beatrice asked. "I mean, who would want any harm to come to Kassie?"

Jake shrugged. "There may be no direct threat, if so my job is just that much easier."

"And if there was a threat?"

"I'd do my best to neutralize it," he replied to Jason.

"So does that make you feel safe?" Jason asked Kassie.

"You bet it does." She looked at Jake. He made her feel safe.

"You must have some things at the house you'd like to take with you," her grandfather said. "I changed nothing in your room."

Kassie looked at her grandfather, considering the offer.

"Maybe," she acknowledged. "I wouldn't mind having that photo of my mom and dad and me the summer before they died." It was the one thing she'd regretted not taking when she'd fled so many years ago. Otherwise, there was nothing in that house she wanted.

"Come anytime and get it. And anything else you want," he said.

She glanced at Jake. "Maybe tomorrow?"

The judged looked crestfallen for a moment, then rallied. "I'll be working all tomorrow, an important case. But Beatrice will be there."

"I have my garden club's Christmas in the Garden event, did you forget? I'll be gone most of the day."

"I don't need anyone there," Kassie said.

"No, I suppose not. Your room is just as you left it," the judge said. "You'll be able to find anything you want."

"Rosalie will be there to let you in," Beatrice added.

"Rosalie is still there?" Kassie smiled in memory of the maid and cook who had worked for her grandfather as long as she could remember. The woman had to be as old as he was—and still keeping house for the family. Amazing.

"I'm sure she'd be delighted to see you," Beatrice said dryly.

Kassie knew her aunt was a bit of a snob. Unlike her mother, who had not had anyone work for her. She always said if she couldn't do for herself, it didn't need doing. But others in the south sometimes felt differently.

"Maybe I'll come by in the morning."

"I'll tell Rosalie to expect you," her grandfather said.

"Tell me more about your school," Betty said after an awkward pause.

Kassie glanced at her grandfather and turned to his new fiancée. "I love teaching. I was fortunate to get this job without much of a background check, because you know where that would have left me."

She remembered how wary she'd been using Sophie's credentials, and how grateful the school had been to get someone of her caliber. She talked about the children she'd taught and cautiously told a little about her friends at the school. The rest of her life in Winter Creek she glossed over. She wouldn't reveal all. She still didn't trust this truce.

"It sounds cold there," Betty said.

"Not much more than here," Kassie replied. "I

remember plenty of snowy days in Atlanta when I was a child."

"Colorado is nothing like Atlanta in winter," Jake murmured.

Everyone laughed.

The evening wound down and Kassie was the first to jump up when the check had been paid.

"Thank you," she said to the group in general.

Jake rose when she did. "I take it we're leaving," he murmured.

"Dinner's done," she replied, anxious to escape the awkward gathering and reach the safety of her motel room.

"Will we see you again before you leave?" Betty asked, with a reassuring glance at the judge.

"I'm not sure. I have to get home before the Christmas break is over. It's a three day drive depending on the weather."

"Stay another couple of days, Kassie. I've missed you," the judge said.

"I'll have to see," she prevaricated. There was no way she was staying.

Once she and Jake were in the jeep, she let out a huge breath. "Whew, that went on forever." She shook her head and inserted the key. The engine roared to life a moment later.

"He was trying, Kassie. I think you need to reassess your view of things. I don't think he tried to kill you." He leaned his head against the back of the seat and closed his eyes. "In thinking about things, you'd probably be safer with him now that he can't benefit from your death than you are with me. Haley still has someone hunting me, as today's bombing proves."

She bit her lip. She had forgotten to tell the judge that she had a will. It seemed awkward to just blurt it out. She glanced at Jake.

"How are you doing?"

"My head aches, vision's just a tad blurry. I'll live." He didn't open his eyes, but kept them closed the entire ride to the motel. Kassie glanced at him from time to time, worried. This was not the intrepid bounty hunger she'd encountered in Colorado or even years earlier in Philadelphia. This man was seriously injured and hiding it the best he could. Two blows to the head in such a short time couldn't be good.

When they reached the motel, there was a light on in their room.

Jake motioned her to stay with the car as he approached the door from the side. He drew his gun, startling her. She didn't know he'd brought it to dinner. Maybe her bodyguard was serious about watching out for her even if he didn't fully believe what she said.

He knocked lightly on the door and it went wide open. Brianna and Thunder stood in the doorway, her hand on his collar. His tail wagged.

"What are you doing here?" Jake asked, putting his gun in the small of his back.

"Got some updates on Haley, John knew you'd want to hear it tonight, so I came by and decided to wait for you. Thunder's good company, aren't you boy?" she said with an affectionate rub of his ears. He wagged his tail again.

In a flash, he took off across the parking lot to run up to Kassie.

"So you didn't forsake me for another," she said with a grin, giving him a hug. "Let's go walk," she said, taking him to the grassy area beneath the motel sign while Jake and Brianna conferred. Once the dog was finished, she headed for her room. Sleep sounded like the best thing right now.

Brianna called a good night to Kassie and jumped into her car. By the time Kassie was inside with the door locked behind her, Brianna had left.

Jake was in the bathroom, brushing his teeth. She listened a moment, wondering what it would be like to live with someone, to know when they were brushing their teeth or taking a bath, or chilling in front of the fire. To know there was someone in her corner no matter what.

She might never know. But given another day or two, she could imagine Jake was just like that.

He came out of the bathroom wearing a towel around his neck and the dress slacks he'd worn to dinner. "I'm heading for bed," he said.

"Gotcha," she said, gathering warm sweats to take into the bathroom. By the time she was ready for bed, Jake was sound asleep. No mattress on the floor tonight.

She climbed into her bed and reached for the light, pausing a moment to study the sleeping man. He looked exhausted. She could see the edge of the bandage on the back of his head. For a moment she wanted to reach out and brush her fingers against his cheek, brush the errant hair from his forehead. Touch him.

She studied him for a long moment, then snapped off the light.

Lying in the dark, she let her mind go over every minute of the evening. Things had gone better than she expected. She wondered if Jake was right. Had a serious of incidents convinced her of something sinister that wasn't truly there?

Could her grandfather have truly wanted her dead for the money he'd get if she died first?

She could hear Jake's even breathing. Smiling into the dark, she relaxed and drifted to sleep enjoying the fantasy a little longer that she had someone in her life that cared.

At breakfast the next morning, Kassie finished eating before broaching the subject of visiting her grandfather's home. "I do want the photo of me and my parents I left behind. But that's all I want."

"Let me check in with John to see where we stand and I'll go with you."

"No need. I'll take Thunder. With grandfather in court all day, there'll be no danger."

"Are you forgetting the two hired men at your place in Colorado?" he asked, taking a sip of milk, having sworn off caffeine until his headache went away.

"After your house blew up yesterday, I'm more leaning to your theory that it is Haley after you and his goons found you at my place."

"Which is what I kept telling you."

"Okay, so maybe you were right. Maybe I read things wrong six years ago. But I've done okay in life."

"And now you can do a lot better, with the money you have inherited."

"I'm still a teacher at Winter Creek Academy and have a classroom of kids to get back to."

"So you are going back? You'll continue to teach?" he asked.

"Why wouldn't I? I love it."

"I want to run by John's for a moment then I'll go with you," Jake said again.

"Really, I'll be fine. I'll swing by the house and pick up the picture, say hi to Rosalie and be back here before you get done with John and Brianna. Then I really do have to make plans for getting home. Can you believe all that's happened over Christmas break? I'll get back home and with some luck no one will ever know I was gone except Stephen."

"And your insurance agent who has written a claim so your house can get repaired."

She blew out a breath in exasperation. "Okay, so half the town will know. But not my kids."

"Not your kids," he agreed, watching her.

"What?"

"I'm just wondering what to make of it all. An heiress working with a bunch of snotty nose kids."

"They're my snotty nose kids and I love every one of them—including Jimmy Doyle, the biggest trouble maker in my class this year."

"Maybe I should have a talk with Jimmy," Jake

suggested.

She laughed. "Like you'll ever come back to Colorado—especially in winter."

"You never know," he said.

Kassie slowed in front of the large old home and stopped her jeep. The tall columns gave it a southern mansion feel, thought it was an eclectically built home spanning several generations. Her grandfather had lived here most of his adult life, purchasing the place when he and his wife were first married and he won his first big case. The home fit their lifestyle.

She remembered coming often with her parents. The laughter that rang out at parties. The fun she'd had in the expansive yard. She didn't remember her grandmother very well. She'd been so young when she'd died. But for a moment her mind dwelt on happy memories, her daddy larger than life, her mother laughing, always smiling. That's how she remembered her.

She let Thunder out of the car and watched him run around the grass, lifting a leg here and there to mark his passing. She rang the doorbell and turned to greet Rosalie when she opened the door.

"Well, I declare if it isn't Miss Sarah. Chile, let me look at you! You are a sight for sore eyes!" The diminutive housekeeper gave her a hard hug which Kassie returned full force.

Tears flooded. "Oh, Rosalie, it's so good to see you," she whispered, not trusting her voice.

The woman held her arms and studied her face. "None of those tears unless they be happy ones. I declare you look brown as a berry in the dead of winter. Where have you been all this time?"

"Colorado," Kassie responded. It was mostly true and saved a long explanation.

"Well, come in, come in. The judge done told me you'd be here today looking into your room. Good think he did so I could fix some of my molasses cookies you like so much."

"On, no, really? Fabulous!" Kassie gave her a big smile. Just the thought of Rosalie's melt-in-your mouth cookies had her mouth watering.

"And who's this fine fellow?" Rosalie asked when Thunder dashed over and sniffed at her apron.

"This is Thunder. He's mine."

"What a beautiful dog. Hey, Thunder, how are you?" She held out her hand. When he ducked his head beneath it, she reached back and scratched his ears. "Well you are a beauty. And you know what, I have some soup bones I was saving for a nice pot of soup, but I bet you'd be a lot more appreciative." She looked at Kassie, "Okay for him to have one?"

"Sure. I want to run upstairs and check out my room then I'll join you in the kitchen."

"Where I'd best be heading or those cookies will burn. Take your time, girl. Come on with me, Thunder, I'll get you that nice soup bone. I declare it's good to have you home again, Miss Sarah."

Kassie entered the house slowly, listening to Rosalie talk to Thunder as they made their way to the back of the house where the large country kitchen was located. Slowly she looked around, closing the front door behind her.

The house was as she remembered. She looked into the living room, a place alive with memories. Christmas with her parents, Aunt Beatrice and Uncle Samuel and Aunt Evelyn and her father all laughing at childhood memories. And of her grandfather enjoying the family gatherings as much as his children and their families had.

The dining room also looked the same. It was a favorite room where huge family meals were held at special occasions from Thanksgiving to birthdays, or a new software design release from her father. The pain in her heart pierced. She missed her parents so much. Those happy days would never come again.

Shaking off her nostalgia, she hurried up the broad curving stairs to the large second floor. A veranda ran outside the windows of the rooms on the front— including the room that had been hers when she'd come to live with her grandfather and Aunt Beatrice after her parent's death.

She opened the door to her room and stepped inside. Nothing had changed just as Aunt Beatrice had said. Everything looked the same as it had the day she left eight years ago.

For a moment she let herself just stand and examine everything she saw. The frilly bed set that Aunt Beatrice had insisted would cheer her up when she was desolate from her parents' death. The bulletin board with notes and receipts still pinned on. The stash of books on the bedside table. And the picture of her parents and her taken that last weekend before the accident.

Going on impulse, she took out her phone and snapped some pictures. She didn't plan to come this way again, but maybe someday in the future, she'd want to remember. Switching to video, she stepped in and panned the room, crossing to the window to scan the view. The manicured lawn, the beds of plants that would flower so colorfully in the spring–so neat and manicured, and in stark contrast to her home in Colorado.

She was about finished when she heard a noise behind her. Dropping her hand, she turned.

"Aunt Beatrice," she said, surprised to see her. "I thought you were at your garden club today."

"I am. Dozens of people have seen me. No one knows I slipped away."

Kassie frowned. What would it matter if they did?

Suddenly she was staring at a gun in her aunt's hand. She registered how small it was, yet knew how deadly. Her aunt wore prim white gloves. It seemed surreal.

In her other hand was a glass of water.

"What's going on?" she asked. When Beatrice didn't speak immediately, Kassie began to hope her aunt didn't realize she still held her phone in her hand. Slowly she slipped her hand behind her, hoping the video was still going. How long could a phone record?

"This time there will be no mistakes," Beatrice said.

"This time?"

Her aunt held out the glass, placing it on the dresser

near Kassie, then stepping back. "Drink the water, Sarah."

"I told you, call me Kassie now. And I'm not thirsty."

"Stupid girl, drink the damn water!" Beatrice glared at her, the gun never wavering.

"No."

"It'll make it easier all around if you do," Beatrice said. She pulled open the shallow drawer in a occasional table by the door and withdrew a syringe.

Kassie had a bad feeling about the entire scenario. Had her aunt gone crazy?

"I'm not drinking the water and I'm not letting you stick me with that syringe."

Suddenly she knew.

"You were the one who drugged me, weren't you?"

No, that couldn't be right. Her aunt had come to take care of her.

"If you had gone with them like you should have, everything would have worked out perfectly. But no, you had to have a cold and stay home."

"What are you talking about?" Kassie asked.

Then she knew. The night her parents had the accident, Kassie had been planning to go with them, but stayed home due to a summer cold. Yet Beatrice couldn't mean the car crash was planned.

Could she?

"You tampered with their car?" Kassie asked in disbelief.

"Child's play when you've grown up with a father and brother obsessed with cars. They never wanted me along, but I picked up all they knew and they never suspected."

"That means you damaged the breaks on my car that time. But why?"

"Drink the water and stop talking," Beatrice said, motioning with the gun.

"No," Kassie said. "If you're planning to kill me, you'll have to shoot. Then there will be a huge investigation and someone will finger you." Her heart was pounding so hard she feared it would burst. Why hadn't she waited for Jake? If she could stall long enough, would Rosalie come looking for her?

"Do you think I'm stupid? I have a perfect alibi, not that anyone would ever think I could have anything to do with a junkie niece's overdose. A dozen women at the garden club saw me this morning. I made sure of that. The event is spread over Sally Felder's entire back and side yard, with a hundred people there. No one can keep track of every one every minute."

"Someone saw you drive way."

"I took the gardener's cart. If anyone saw it, they'd think Sally's gardener was going to get another plant for her. You're stalling and I don't have time for this." Her voice rang with frustration.

"Killing me won't get you anything," Kassie said desperately. She wished she could check the phone, but she dare not give any hint to her aunt. If she was killed, her only hope was the phone would provide evidence of her killer.

"There are laws in Georgia on who inherits what. I don't get it all, but I'll get enough as a sibling of your father," Beatrice said.

"Except I signed the papers at the bank, and I left a will," Kassie said.

Beatrice stared at her. "What did you say?"

"Jake told me before we got here about my inheritance. I went to the bank yesterday, set up payment to my bank. I signed all the papers that transferred everything to me. I wrote a will before we got here–leaving any and everything of which I die possessed to my friend in Colorado."

Beatrice stared at her as if trying to understand the words.

"How could you have left all that money to a stranger?" she screamed in outrage.

"Eileen isn't a stranger. She's my friend," Kassie said, wondering how she could get away from her aunt. Her heart pounded. She wished she'd waited for Jake as he'd asked her.

"We're talking millions of dollars! It belongs to your family, not some person you met in the last couple of years."

"Except that's exactly what I did." Kassie gaze flicked around the room. Her aunt blocked the door. Could she make it out onto the veranda and escape? Not if Beatrice was any kind of marksman.

" Let me think." She glared at Kassie for a moment in blind rage, "Damn, I had it all planned, since you showed up again. If you'd stayed hidden, you would have been declared dead."

Kassie narrowed her eyes. "You took the note I left, didn't you? You took the money grandfather thought was going to the kidnapers."

"I needed that money. My son needed that money. You were going to inherit millions and I lived off the charity of my father. He was so surprised when you didn't show up after he paid. I should have asked for more."

"You should not have lied to him and everyone," Kassie said, then thought how dumb that sounded. If her aunt had murdered two people, a little lying would hardly make a blimp on her moral radar.

Beatrice slowly smiled. "You'll simply have to write another will. Say you realize since coming home how much your family means to you. Leave it all to me and Jason. Look in the desk, there's bound to still be some paper there."

"And if I refuse? You'll shoot?"

Beatrice narrowed her eyes. "Believe it. I'll shoot one knee out, and then the other, and then an elbow if you don't comply." The muzzle dropped slightly and Kassie knew Beatrice wouldn't hesitate to carry out her threat.

Kassie stepped closer, dropping her phone on the dresser as she reached for the water. She had no intention of drinking, nor letting her aunt shoot her, but until something gave, they were at an impasse and she could see Beatrice was growing more and more agitated. She hoped her aunt's frustration kept her from registering the phone.

Drink it!" Beatrice ordered.

Kassie raised the glass to her lips, then flung it toward her aunt the glass and water flying into Beatrice's face.

Beatrice ducked and swung the gun up and fired. The bullet passed so close Kassie could swear she felt its heat.

From downstairs she heard her dog bark and knew she only had to wait for Thunder to find her and Beatrice was toast. But could she keep from being killed until then?

She dived across the bed as a second gunshot sounded. This one went wild, at least she hope it had as she rolled off the bed on the far side, scrambling to keep the bed between them.

Suddenly she heard the deep familiar growl and one hundred ten pounds of attack-trained German Shepherd launched into the room and locked his jaws around the wrist of the hand that held a gun.

Beatrice screamed.

Kassie peered over the bed. Thunder growled and shook the arm until the gun dropped, then he remained still, his mouth still biting Beatrice's arm, his growling low and fierce. He tugged on her arm as she screamed and hit him again and again in an attempt to make him let go. But his training held. The dog did not release her.

Shaken, Kassie rose from behind the bed and came around. She kicked the gun across the room and reached out to touch Thunder's shoulder.

"Lenye," she said firmly. He opened his mouth, released the screaming woman and lay down, his eyes still fixed on Beatrice.

Rosalie came flying in through the door.

"What in the world is going on?"

"That dog attacked me. Get him away! Get him away!" Beatrice screamed scurrying back away from Thunder.

The dog glanced at Kassie and then resumed watching Beatrice. One wrong move from her, one word from Kassie, and he'd attack again.

Two seconds later Jake appeared in the doorway, gun in hand. It took less than two seconds for him to assess the situation.

"It wasn't your grandfather, it was your aunt," he said.

Kassie nodded, still numb from the events of the last few minutes. "And she killed my mom and dad, too," she said in disbelief as she went around the end of the bed, crossed the room and went straight into his arms. He tightened his hold, giving her a feeling of safety. She couldn't believe all that had happened. Blood pounded in her veins. Her breathing felt constricted. She clung to Jake, wishing she could rewind the clock and never come to Atlanta.

Yet, she now knew the truth. It hadn't been her grandfather after all.

"It's all lies. From a crazy in the head girl who should never have been let out of a mental hospital. Rosalie, call me an ambulance and get these people out of my home!" Beatrice screamed. She moaned, cradling her injured arm against her chest.

"The house belongs to the judge, Miss Beatrice, and I figure he'll tell me who to get rid of and who not to. I'll call an ambulance for you." Rosalie turned and left.

"And the cops, while you're at it," Jake added as Kassie half turned to look at her aunt, still from the safety of Jake's arms.

Beatrice held her bleeding wrist cradled against her chest, the gloves she wore both soaked in blood. The woolen suit discolored with blood.

Thunder hadn't moved. He continued to watch her every breath.

"Get that dog out of here," she snapped. "I'll sue. He attacked me in my own home. He's a menace and needs to be put down!"

"No, where I go, Thunder goes. He saved my life," Kassie explained to Jake.

"I told you to wait for me."

"What brought you at the right time?" she asked, still staring at her aunt in disbelief.

"Right time? Seems like you had it all wrapped up, thanks to your dog."

"I'm still really glad to see you. She wanted me to drink some water and then planned to shoot me up with drugs, I think. The water's probably drugged. She was trying to make it seem like an overdose, but how she expected to get anyone to believe it after seeing me last night I don't know."

"Get out," Beatrice screamed.

Jake shook his head. "We'll wait right here with you for the police and the paramedics."

"You won't find my fingerprints on anything," Beatrice said triumphantly.

Jake nodded, looking at the gloves still on her hands. "I expect not. Which is telling, isn't it. If Kassie really shot up, her fingerprints would be on the syringe. Since she never touched it, I guess you know what that tells us."

"My father will never believe you. I'm his daughter. You're just some two-bit private investigator he hired. And you've probably fallen for a pretty face. Men always do. Get out."

Jake replaced his gun at the small of his back.

"Are you sure you don't need that anymore?" Kassie asked.

"Thunder makes sure of that. You're safe now, Kassie. And I expect you never have to fear for your life again. "

She sagged against him for a second, relishing the strength of his arms. Then she pushed back a bit. "All along I thought it was my grandfather. But it wasn't. How could I have been so blind?"

"You should have died all those years ago. The money just sat in the bank. I needed that money. Now more than ever," Beatrice snarled. She struggled to her feet, raising her head high. "I'm going to my room."

Sirens could be heard in the distance

"No." Jake said. "You're staying right here until the authorities arrive. Which from the sound of things, shouldn't be too long now."

It was after seven o'clock that evening before the last forensic specialist and police officer left. Judge Sutherland and Betty sat in the living room with Jake, John and Kassie. Thunder had been examined by the crime lab and while the recommendation had been to turn him over to animal control for observation and quarantine, Judge Sutherland had prevailed and the dog was in the kitchen with Rosalie gnawing on the soup bone she'd given him earlier.

Kassie couldn't look at her grandfather without guilt threatening to overwhelm her. All these years she'd thought he tried to kill her. He had never done so. She'd been so sure. Beatrice had fooled them all.

He looked years older than he had yesterday.

Betty sat beside him, holding his hand, patting it gently with her other hand.

John and Jake stood near the window talking in low voices.

Rosalie came to the archway "I have dinner on the table. Good pot roast and all the fixens. Y'all come and eat now, y'hear?"

"I'm not hungry," the judge said.

"Nonsense, Judge. You gotta keep yourself up and going. This is not the end of the world. You've had worse. No one died today. Come on now and eat. Miss Betty, you tell your man to get up and get some food in him."

Betty smiled and nodded, standing and tugging him up. "She's right, Martin. We need to eat. Tomorrow is time enough to deal with everything. Tonight is just family."

Once they were served and began eating, the judge put down his fork and looked at Kassie.

"My dear, I'm so sorry. All along you thought someone was trying to kill you and you were right. Only I never suspected. I was convinced you were imagining things or being overly dramatic.

"You had it from both sides, though, Judge," Jake said. "Beatrice was constantly reassuring you and giving reasons for Kassie's wild accusations which made you think she was crazy."

"But to kill Jonathan and Jane. That I can't fathom," the older man said sadly. "Her own brother, it doesn't make sense."

"Why would she?" Betty asked.

Jake glanced around the group. "Their deaths came shortly after her husband left her. I think she was afraid of the future. You, if I'm correct, Judge, did not approve of her marriage and weren't sympathetic when the man proved to be no good and left. I don't think Beatrice was prepared to make it on her own as a single mother. She thought with Jonathan gone, the money would be divided between you, her and Samuel. She referenced intestacy laws when threatening Kassie."

"She killed her brother for money?" Judge Sutherland shook his head in disbelief.

"We may never know the full ins and outs," Jake said. "She's remaining firm in her statement that Kassie made it all up. Fortunately the recording Kassie made, while showing only the carpet on the floor, has her voice clear and sharp. Every damning word came through."

"She was the cutest little girl. Lillian doted on her," the judge said of his late wife.

"She's still your daughter," Kassie said. "She'll need you in the months and years ahead. Whether she gets jail time or psychiatric treatment."

"She's not crazy," the judge protested.

Jake glanced at Kassie. No softening the truth for the old man.

"I'll see to her defense, but I will also uphold the law. It's been my touchstone all my life," the judge said.

Kassie nodded. "I'm sorry I thought you tried to kill me," she said softly.

"I'm sorry I didn't believe what you were saying years ago. Sorry I even sent for Beatrice in the first place," her grandfather replied.

For a long moment there was only silence. Than Jake spoke, "My suggestion to you both is play catch up for the day or two Kassie has left before she has to get back to her school. There will be time enough to hash everything out in the days and weeks ahead. Time now to finish dinner."

"You just want some of Rosalie's molasses cookies," Kassie said with a surprising laugh, "which is why we need to eat up now." Her heart felt free for the first time in years. The threat was truly gone. Her life was her own.

She grinned at Jake and wondered if he'd ever consider a ski trip to Colorado.

Epilogue

The car pulled into the clearing and stopped facing the cabin door.

Thunder whined and went to the door and Kassie followed, curious as to who had come to see her. She was in the middle of a good mystery and hated to put it down, so whoever was interrupting better have a good reason.

School had been out three days and she was lazing around like summer would last forever. Maybe it was one of the appeals of being a teacher, but she loved the long days with nothing to do but whatever she wanted.

She opened the door and stood in the doorway, watching as the man climbed out of the car. Her heart began to race. The smile on her face couldn't be contained. Skype had nothing on the real thing.

Thunder raced down the stairs as she watched him wait for the dog to run up. He gave him a pet then looked up at her.

She didn't need the shotgun this time, though it still stood by the door. So much had changed since that fateful Christmas break.

The cabin had been repaired last winter and looked

as nice as it ever had. Her car had been replaced, Stephan's jeep returned. There was little evidence of the gun assault that changed her life.

"What brings you by?" she called as if he were a neighbor stopping in on the way home from town. She wanted to run into his arms, feel them tighten around her. She wanted his kiss in the wort way. But she tried for a nonchalant look, hoping he couldn't see her heart banging away so hard in her chest she hoped it wouldn't explode.

"Thought I'd see what Colorado looks like in summer," he said, walking toward her. His eyes never left hers. That half smile she loved in evidence. "And see how your disposition was in warmer weather."

"My disposition's always been fine."

"Sometimes gunshots go off around you which seemed to make you cranky." The teasing tone was in direct contrast to the hard contours of his face. She wasn't afraid of Jake one little bit—not any more.

"Sometimes cranky is deserved." She smiled, her heart beginning to beat even faster. He looked good. Amazingly good. And if he didn't give her a clue in the next five seconds, she was going to say to hell with being nonchalant and jump his bones.

He stopped by the bottom of the steps. "You granddad and Betty will be along in another month," he said.

"So I heard. And that they had a lovely wedding in April. I almost went."

"You would have liked it."

"So you said at the time. I can't believe you went."

"Representing you," he said, stepping up on the stairs, coming right up to her so she had to tilt back her head to see him.

"I heard they sold the old family home and bought a snazzy condo which Betty's decorated from top to bottom," she said, reaching out to touch his arm, just to make sure he was real.

"Your aunt got life in prison," he said, his hands coming up to cradle her face, his eyes flicking from hers to her lips and back again.

"I heard that, too. Better than a needle, I guess. Grandfather is trying to make up for the havoc she caused in our lives." She didn't have a lot of compassion for the woman who had killed her parents, depriving her of them for most of her life. Cut theirs short ruthlessly.

"We caught up with Haley," he leaned closer, his breath brushing across her cheeks

"Brianna told me."

If he didn't kiss her in about two seconds--

"So, are you here to give Colorado another try?" she asked, wishing her heart would stop pounding so hard.

"Nope, I'm here to convince you to return to Atlanta?" he countered, giving her a half smile before his lips covered hers in a soul-searing kiss.

They had talked for hours on Skype. Sometimes on the phone. This conversation told her nothing new, but his kisses were hot and passionate. And so very welcomed after the months apart.

"Are you here to take me back?" she asked breathlessly a few minutes later when Jake pulled back a fraction and rested his forehead on hers..

"It would be lots easier now than in the dead of winter." He looked at her again. "But I'd rather you come on your own. We have some fine schools in Atlanta crying out for good teachers. It would give you time to get to know your grandfather better. And be there for Jason."

She thought it over. "He's hurting, isn't he? I know how impossible it was for me to believe she did all that, how awful for him to know his mother is a killer."

"In situations like this, family rallies around. Come rally around your famiy."

"And you?"

"Maybe something might develop that would include me in your family," he said, drawing her into his arms and kissing her again. Kassie knew she could only hold out for another few minutes. She'd already given her notice to the school. Made plans to move after her grandfather and Betty visited. She wanted to show off where she'd lived, but was ready to return to Atlanta— with Jake. Trusting him and knowing their future would be bright and happy.

Thunder sat and cocked his head at the two locked in an embrace. He didn't sense any danger.